HOME

Alyanna Poe
New Year's Eve 2025

Dedicated to my chronically ill friends.
Even if we've never met,
I see you.

One

Oh my God, his profile picture must be from ten years ago.

In the photos she'd seen of him, he had rich brown hair kept sharply cut and a constant five-o'clock shadow. His skin was flawless, and he knew how to dress. He looked like he smelled of cologne and possibly expensive cigars.

The man standing before Charlotte had unkempt mousey gray hair, and the stubble on his face was patchy and long in odd places. His clothing was wrinkled, seeming as if he had just pulled them from a pile, and he smelled *nothing* like cologne or expensive cigars.

"Hey, it's so good to finally see you in person," she said. She hugged him, keeping her body from fully pressing into his. Her eyes stared into themselves from the reflection in the tinted cafe windows, begging her to leave. She cringed, wondering if this was a good idea.

"Yeah, you look so much prettier than your photos," he said, face buried in her hair. He deeply inhaled, clutching her tightly.

She stumbled forward as he pulled her in, clumsily bumping into him in a full-bodied hug. She laughed and held her arms out away from him, waiting for him to release her. After seconds of gut-wrenching awkwardness, he finally let go. Both of them sighed, hers being shakier than his.

Jeff opened the door to the cafe, letting her in under his arm and following closely behind.

After ordering, the two sat in a booth nestled in the corner of the room. Loud voices and laughter echoed off the tiled floor and the walls, rattling her already overwhelmed mind. She stared at the floor, certain Jeff's gaze was directly on her.

She pulled her attention from the tile at her feet, a dull throbbing in the back of her head. His dark eyes gave her more anxiety than the cafe's loud patrons. She attempted to smile, feeling the way her lips tightened around her teeth in a grimace rather than a relaxed smile.

"How's the painting been?" he asked.

She shrugged. "The muse has not been kind."

Elbow on the table, he leaned his chin on his hand. "I wish I could be that muse."

She fended off the heebie-jeebies. "Yeah," she said, and chuckled.

"You brought the painting I asked for, right?"

She nodded, thinking of the painting in the backseat of her car. "Yeah. I'm surprised you wanted that one." It was one of her earlier pieces, one she wasn't impressed with.

"Well, I wouldn't have noticed the painting if it weren't for the beautiful woman holding it in the photo."

The statement stung. Charlotte already knew she was pretty. She didn't need that reinforced. Painting was her *passion*. At times, painting was her everything. Her skillset was more important to her than his opinion on her looks.

Their names were called, somehow traveling to their table over the raucous laughter of the table next to theirs. She shot out of the booth, followed by Jeff, who appeared unbothered by the noise.

Grabbing his cup, he asked, "Want to go outside?"

She looked around with strikingly wide eyes and nodded, her headache mounting into sharp, jagged pains. She usually avoided public places at peak hours, opting to stay home in her studio. Her quiet, sunny studio. She'd open a window and let the breeze in. Birds might chirp as she painted.

Landscapes were her specialty. Portraits rarely interested her.

He laughed as they walked through the door. "You really don't like crowds, do you?"

It irked her that he found her discomfort funny. She shrugged off the question, noticing all the outdoor tables were full.

"We can sit on my tailgate," he said.

She looked up at him, her gaze trailing the crepey skin around his mouth and eyes as he smiled. When he had asked to buy one of her paintings, she'd been honored. When he had asked to meet for coffee to discuss art, she was thrilled. He could've been a door to other buyers, or even a gallery feature if he knew the right people. Charlotte learned early on that it's all about networking if you want to make a living as an artist. Further into their first conversation, when he asked if she was single, her excitement had lessened. This wasn't a meet and greet. It was a coffee date. Based on his photos, she had expected someone closer in age to her, someone she could *potentially* find attractive. She was twenty-three, and he had to be at least her father's age.

At least.

Slurping up the whipped cream off the top of her drink with her straw, she said, "Sure."

He led her to his small blue pickup, opened the tailgate, and presented it graciously.

She set her drink on it and wiped some dirt from the spot she planned to sit. Using both hands to hop up, she plopped onto it and dangled her legs. The parking lot was full, but everyone appeared to be somewhere inside the small shopping plaza. She glanced back at him, picking up her coffee. Sipping it, she asked, "When did you say you're moving?"

His smile weakened, and his eyes took on a hardened look. "Soon," he said just under his breath.

Charlotte's skin crawled as he stood close. She set her hand down on the metal to scoot over just as his hand fell over hers.

His eyes bore deeply into hers, a faint smile on his lips. "Soon, sweetheart."

A shiver spread across her skin, starting at the base of her neck. She looked down at her coffee, taking another sip without noticing the splash of white powder on top of the whipped cream. Her heart raced under his gaze as she nervously stirred it all together.

"So, you live alone?" he asked, breaking a tense silence.

She snapped a look up to him, shaking her head. "No, no. I live with my parents and younger brother."

"Oh." He sipped on his iced tea. "You said you're in college, right?"

Charlotte nodded.

"What are you studying?" He stepped closer to her.

Feeling his breath beating down on her, she said, "Visual arts."

"Ah, so you *are* sticking with painting." He laughed and winked.

She took a big drink, her nose scrunching as she swallowed a mouthful of caramel syrup. "You're a pharmacist?"

He jumped. "Who said that?"

"You did, the other night."

He shook his head, eyes wide. "No, no. I'm a, a uh, farm technician. I work with…horses." He swallowed the rest of his tea, grimacing. As Charlotte opened her mouth to speak, he spoke first. "So, what do you like to do for fun?"

She shrugged, thinking of the stack of books in the corner of her room. "I *read.*"

Jeff scoffed. "Well, that's not very fun."

She shrugged again. She mostly read books about art history, and when she did read fiction, it was still historical. She could talk about techniques and styles and time periods for hours, but she knew he wouldn't care. He would nod along or talk over her.

Redundancy at its best.

"I'm sure we can figure out something fun to do." He gently pushed a strand of golden hair behind her ear, smiling. "Moving is going to be hard, but it'll be worth it."

She wanted to say something but couldn't form the words in her mouth. They sat scrambled in her head as she looked out at the parking lot. Images of books and paintings and the bucket of wet brushes she knew she needed to clean flashed through her mind, much like that rush of thoughts one gets before falling asleep.

Finally, she nodded, slowly, just to acknowledge what he said. She took the last sip of her coffee. It was incredibly bitter, and her stomach hurt. She wondered why she had agreed to this impromptu *date*.

Empty cup in hand, she gave a weak smile while he droned on about how hard the drive was going to be. If she could just get a word in, she would let him know she was going to be late to her mother's pap smear or the rapture or anything else, just to leave. She would lie until her pants caught fire if only it meant solitude.

She was tired, like a heavy weight had been set on her. When she blinked, it felt like lifting ten pounds just to open her eyes again. She leaned back, supporting herself with her hand.

His smile grew along with her weariness, and he sat next to her, wrapping an arm about her shoulders.

Her cup slipped from her grasp. She watched it spiral down and smack the asphalt a thousand miles below her feet. The lid popped off the cup, spraying coffee-coated ice across the darkness. Looking up at Jeff made her queasy. His closeness frightened her, but she was too exhausted to move away. The way his smile continually crept wider, squinting his eyes further, terrified her, and on top of it, the wild, disordered gray hair seemed to slip further and further away from his forehead with every slow word.

She closed her eyes, falling limply in his arms.

Two

Charlotte's eyes fluttered open. First in her line of sight were her legs, curled up on an old bench seat in the cab of a truck she didn't recognize. She gasped, looking out at a gas station and people bustling around the truck. Her eyes locked onto the sign above the convenience store.

Richie's: The Best Prices in All of Utah.

Utah?

Her heart thudded.

I live in California.

Her limbs felt heavy, like her bones weighed an extra fifty pounds, but that didn't stop her from unbuckling and opening the door. Through the glass of the gas station's convenience store, she could see Jeff at the register, his hair even further back on his head.

It's a wig.

This gave her pause. She'd heard of toupees and such, but she questioned why Jeff would pick such a ratty wig for a first date.

This stupid train of thought ate seconds, giving Jeff the opportunity to turn and see her hanging out of the truck.

Charlotte's eyes widened. She threw herself to the ground, her knees almost giving way, and ran. Her feet slapped the asphalt as she booked it across the parking lot and into the busy street. She didn't know where she was headed, but it certainly had to be better than wherever Jeff was taking her.

Her hip nearly missed the front end of a car, and she stopped in time to miss faceplanting into a panel van. Just as her foot landed on the sidewalk, she could hear Jeff screaming. She ran, ducking and weaving through people. Her hands searched her pockets for her phone, her pocketknife, her *anything*, but came up empty.

Her stomach twisted as she thought about Jeff's dirty fingers rummaging around in her pockets while she was unconscious.

She couldn't run forever, so she took the opportunity to dive into a small café. The door was open and more inviting than the street. Upon busting in, the baristas and a couple sitting at a table gasped. Charlotte bent over, catching her breath when tires squealed in the parking lot.

"Are you okay?" one of the baristas asked.

Charlotte held up a finger, her chest burning.

What a time to *not* have an inhaler handy.

Footsteps thundered into the café and out of the corner of her eye, she saw Jeff in the doorway.

Foaming at the mouth like a rabid dog, he shouted, *"Get in the truck!"*

Without a second thought, Charlotte sprinted for the back of the café, slamming into the double doors which housed the kitchen. She dodged a woman carrying cinnamon rolls and took a left. Avoiding the freezer door which popped open as she passed, she threw herself through the back door, catching two baristas on a smoke break off guard.

Jeff, seemingly stuck in the kitchen, hadn't caught up with her.

She took a second to look around, spotting a police station across the street, shining like a beacon of hope in the afternoon sun. Charlotte ran for it, unaware that she'd already been a missing person for over 24 hours.

Out in broad daylight, as she crossed the busy street, a red car turned the corner, one she'd never seen before. The driver, bald, gritted his teeth as he fished something out of the passenger seat. He transferred it from his right to his left hand, whipping it out the driver's window.

The collapsible Billy club extended.

Jeff swerved into oncoming traffic to get in front of Charlotte. She screamed, turning away from the car. Jeff swung. The Billy club smashed into the back of her head.

She was unconscious before she hit the asphalt and within seconds, Jeff stopped the car, got out, threw her into the trunk, and was off again, only to be seen by stunned drivers and pedestrians.

In broad daylight, a young woman was abducted yet again.

Three

I think I'm gonna vomit. Why is it so hot in here?

Charlotte flipped onto her side, bile rolling up her throat and into the darkness where she had been stuffed.

She wiped her mouth with a trembling hand and tried to stretch out, confined to a small space. She lost gravity for a moment, smacking her sore head on something before landing harshly.

"*Shit.*"

She was in the trunk of a car, and she felt that they were on the freeway, headed somewhere isolated, no doubt. She reached up, first touching a large, sensitive welt on the back of her head, then wrapping her fingers around a metal bar. Without light, she felt the ends of it, realizing she held a crowbar. She hadn't felt so lucky in a long time.

She got on her hands and knees, forced into a plank position, and ran her fingers along the trunk, finding the groove where the lid met the body. She shoved the crowbar in, and with every ounce of her being, she yanked down, crumpling the lid a small bit. She recoiled, shoving the crowbar in with a thud and pushing harder.

Every impact was a chance for Jeff to hear her, so she worked hard at prying, elated to see a sliver of light. Bracing herself, she shoved the crowbar in as far as possible, pressing her back into the lid. She clasped her hands to her chest, and in a quick, downward swing, she struck the crowbar, popping open the trunk.

Breathless, she smiled at the dusk-pink road trailing away from her. With no cars in sight, and judging the asphalt speeding by to be safer than the man driving, she dove out of the trunk, landing on her back and rolling. She barreled over and over again, wondering if her body would ever stop, before coming to an abrupt halt on her face.

Feeling like she just escaped a blender, she pulled herself to her hands and knees, barely able to drag herself forward. Air scraped through her straw-sized throat.

Squealing tires sounded far ahead of her as red lights lit up the dim road.

She threw one hand in front of the other, hauling her legs behind herself. Her skin felt hot, and as she pulled herself along, she noticed her skinned, bleeding arms. The tall grass on the side of the road would be her only solace as the taillights changed from red to white. Her eyes widened, and despite all the pain in her body, she forced herself to stand, limping into the field.

The car lurched backward just as her knee gave out. She landed on her chest on a heap of dirt, knocking what little air she had out of herself. Pressed to the ground, she crawled under a few thick patches of grass and lay on her side, curling her knees up to her chest.

Deep, slow breaths calmed her as she listened.

A car door slammed, and she could hear Jeff's heavy footfalls across the road, through the gravel, and into the brush.

The sun set fast, leaving little light to be had. Charlotte stared at her hands, balled up against her chest, until something caught her eye.

Inches before her face, a snake slithered by.

A scream rose to her lips, where she clamped it between her teeth. She grimaced as the slick scales shimmered in the dusk, sliding within reach of her nose. A damp, musky smell made her stomach wrench. She knew she had to endure, lest she be found.

Overhead, a flashlight illuminated the brush. She lay trembling as the last of the snake passed by her face, its rattle shiny from the glare of the darting light.

Jeff sighed. He was close enough for her to hear, but his footsteps slowly distanced themselves from her. When his car door slammed, she relaxed into the dirt. The car started and drove off.

She couldn't believe her ears.

Charlotte lay still, wide eyes looking in the direction the snake had gone. Through her crop top and jeans, she could feel the evening chill creeping up from the dirt and trailing down from the misty air. It was about to get colder than she could handle.

Options ran around her mind, back and forth between staying or running. She knew he didn't leave her. He had to be somewhere close by.

She rolled onto her back, sore and most certainly still bleeding. The cool air would later bring cold, inescapable hypothermia, but as she closed her eyes, she let the breeze wash over her. In her mind, she was camping with her family. Maybe playing hide and seek with her brother. She was dirty and in pain, not from running for her life, but from hiking and chopping wood and throwing pinecones. She would see the sun rise tomorrow through the pine needles. It would wash over her and kiss her wounds. Tomorrow would be a new day.

She coughed, fear gripping her body as she hoped he didn't hear her.

Images of him parking on a nearby side road and staring out his car all night with binoculars flashed on her closed eyelids. A clip of him searching the field until he stumbled over her sleeping body and yanked her off the ground by her arm played over and over, and each time she tried to fight him, she lost.

A cricket chirped behind her, causing her eyes to snap open.

She asked herself the big question again, *stay or run?* and rolling onto her stomach, she crawled away from the road. She ducked below the grass and dodged big clumps of it, hoping to give the appearance of stillness across the field. Her elbows quickly became slick with mud, causing her to slip around. She squinted through the dimness, stopping when she saw the figure of something ahead. Although the sun had set and there was nothing but a void above her, Charlotte's eyes gave her the gray images one catches in the dark. The figure stared back at her.

It croaked and hopped into a bush, eliciting a small sigh of relief from her.

She kept crawling, eventually pushing herself over a small hill and into crushed rock. She hissed as her elbow landed on the first of the gravel, and here she would have to make another decision. She cleared the dirt with her hands, pushing away as much jagged rock as she could before crawling forward, and repeated this twice before reaching asphalt. Looking both ways, she saw no lights and pushed herself onto the road. Across the road was another field, full of corn. Tall, stalks of corn that Charlotte was certain she could hide in.

Just as she dragged herself across the halfway point, headlights turned a corner onto the road. They turned night into day as Charlotte struggled to her feet.

The pickup slammed on its brakes, screaming in the quiet air.

She held up her arms, legs glued in place.

"Goddamn it!" The driver swung open his door and landed on the asphalt. Though she couldn't see his face, Charlotte tensed at the anger in his voice. He was a large man. "Don't you know you're on private property?!" he yelled, slamming his door shut and trudging toward her.

Her arms wrapped about her body, and she took a step back, the headlights still obscuring her view of the man. Seconds passed as her mind clambered for words.

Jeff's car rolled in behind her, and words finally came to mind.

"No!"

The large man stopped a few feet in front of her, his gray beard and pocked skin illuminated by Jeff's headlights. His small, beady eyes took her in. He held his hands up in hesitation, like he was cornering a small animal.

"I'm sorry, I didn't know." She pointed to the car, the events leading up to this moment hurdling through her mind.

What if he doesn't believe me?

Who would *believe you?*

Her chest felt on the verge of explosion.

Jeff popped his door and got out. "*Bethany!* Get back in the car!"

She glanced over at him as he approached, her back to the corn field. Looking at the old man, she asked, "Can't you help me?"

"What are you doing with my wife?!" Jeff yelled.

As the old man opened his mouth to speak and his brow furrowed in anger, she bolted for the corn field.

A few strides in, she could hear Jeff behind her. Stumbling through stalks and slippery mud, she ducked to the left. Running gave every nerve in her body a strike of fire as fresh scabs tore open and her lungs fought for air. The corn leaves ripped new wounds into her skin. She tried to keep her breathing even, but as she ran along, her limbs went weak. Her chest tightened.

She stopped, slipping in under a bundle of stalks, and listened.

Silence.

Besides the stalks around her, which rustled gently in the cool breeze. Where she crouched, she could see nothing. No light shone through the corn. She waited, anticipating Jeff's hand bursting through the leaves, grabbing her limbs, and dragging her off.

Carefully, and as quietly as possible, she sat in the mud, curling her knees up to her chest. Every muscle in her body trembled and jittered. As she marinated in the cold silence, her stomach made a debut with a loud growl. Her mind left the present and entered her body. The inside of her mouth was dry, her tongue desperate for any source of moisture. The back of her head throbbed. It felt hot and sickly. Her stomach did flips and turned inside out as it started to gnaw on her other organs. The cold bit through her clothes and into her skin, making her fingers and toes numb. She just wanted to be home. She and her parents and her brother would've ordered pizza. They might've played Scrabble or Just Dance. She would've asked her brother how school was.

What day is it? she wondered.

She would make microwaves s'mores and share. She would shower and brush her hair until she was tired, and she'd fall asleep in her comfy bed in her childhood home with a family that loves her only through the walls.

A hand jutted out of the leaves, landing on the back of her neck. She screamed, only to have another hand cover her lips.

Jeff yanked her back, pulling her through the stalks by her head. Her body, slick with mud, limply slid through the field. She only strained her neck muscles to keep it from breaking.

Jeff dragged her through the field and onto the road before letting go.

"Get up."

Charlotte lay there, facing up at him.

"Why are you doing this to me?" Her voice was soft and sad, stinging him.

He stared down at her, chewing his lip. She was so *young*. Innocent. In the moonlight, her pretty eyes glittered with a fresh onslaught of tears. Tears welled in his own eyes as he scooped her up, but images from his past surfaced, and his face hardened. He stuffed her into the back seat and got in, quickly starting the car and whipping around.

There was a reason for all this madness. A reason that would fix all of his problems.

She stared out the window at the passing cars. She hurt bad, all over. The back of her neck was sticky with many hours' worth of trickling blood. Her entire body was wet and cold. The car's heater couldn't even touch the chill she felt. Eyes burning, she cried, sobbing behind Jeff's head.

He looked in the rearview mirror at her, pity still tugging at his heart. Grabbing an open water bottle from the cupholder, he tried to hand it back to her. "Charlotte, you must be parched."

She looked up from between her wet fingers, face red.

14

He dodged her quick hand, which was aimed at his temple, and kept the drink from spilling. He huffed out a breath. "It's fine," he paused, taking a swig and swallowing, "see?"

She moved her tongue across the roof of her mouth.

His foot hit the accelerator hard as her fist pounded into the side of his head. She recoiled and struck again, causing him to swerve into the median, where he suddenly braked.

She, unbuckled, was sent into the dash from the backseat, crashing onto the center console. She threw her hands at him repeatedly as he slipped a blanket out from under his seat.

Throwing it over her, she tangled up in it quickly, falling into the passenger seat. He snatched a small string of rope from the floorboard of the back seat and grabbed her. Seconds later, her arms were bound down with a cartoon fish blanket cascading over her shoulders and an old piece of dirty rope around her wrists.

Her eyes burned into his, and with what little saliva she had, she spit in his face.

Jeff reached below his seat again, pulling out a funnel with a long neck.

Charlotte's eyes widened, darting between him and the bright-colored funnel. She shook her head, rearing her legs up to push him off.

He grabbed her by the throat, cinching down on it with his large hand.

Her skin flushed red as she kept her mouth shut, his hand cutting off her air. She trembled under his weight, her vision blurring. He let go, and as she gasped, he shoved the funnel in, scraping down her throat. She gagged, trying to force it out with her esophagus as he grabbed the water bottle, somehow unspilled in the cupholder. He dumped the bottle of cloudy liquid into the funnel, watching as she choked on it before relaxing, allowing the tainted water into her stomach.

When the bottle was empty and the funnel drained, he gently removed the neck from her throat, noticing a small smear of blood on the end.

She writhed in her seat, determined to free her hands. Churning her stomach, she forcefully gagged, trying to get the liquid back up. Dry heave after dry heave, the liquid remained heavy in her gut.

Her raw, asphalt eaten arms burned under the restraints, and in a huff, she slammed back into the seat as he got back on the freeway. Throat sore, she wanted to cry, but more than anything, she wanted to be back home. She relaxed in the cushiony seat, embraced by the restraints and the feeling of no control.

Looking over at Jeff only caused more nausea. His twisted smile was at its largest, scrunching his face like the sick monster he was.

The familiar feeling of exhaustion washed over her as she stared at the passing cars, hypnotized. She reached over slowly, her bound hands the weight of a car, and wrapped her fingers around the door handle. She yanked with what little strength she had, finding the door locked. She swiveled her head on her neck like swinging open an old barn door and glared at him through heavy eyes.

He glanced over at her with his own smiling eyes, saying, "Go to sleep now. You'll be up and at 'em soon enough."

She grunted, trembling under the weighted feeling. Hot tears rolled down her cheeks. Gently, she closed her eyes, leaning her head back against the headrest. Taking slow, deep breaths to remain calm, she fell into a deep sleep.

Four

What stinks? Why does my head hurt?

"Beth, you've barely touched your peas."

Charlotte opened her eyes, picking up her head from its painful resting place on her shoulder.

"Oh, Beth, are you feeling alright?"

A bald man sat across the table from her, his soft voice rocking her already throbbing skull.

She blinked her heavy lids at him, looking around the room and down at herself. She recognized none of it. She didn't even recognize herself. She realized the bald man was referring to her as Beth. His eyes struck her as intimidating as he stared at her, fork and knife in hand.

She looked down at her plate, seeing meatloaf and mashed potatoes. She didn't know what the green things were. Unable to say the name, she could still recall a taste.

"Aren't the peas good?" the bald man asked.

She gazed at the mound of round, green things and abruptly stood up, pushing her chair over with a clatter. Swinging her head wildly, she looked for any exit. The vibrant red front door soundlessly screamed at her. She took a step forward only to be pulled off her feet.

"Beth. *Bethany!*" The man held her from behind, keeping her arms at her sides. "Please stop!" Despite yelling, his voice sounded sad.

Charlotte flailed in his arms. She opened her mouth to scream when his hand clamped over her lips, painfully smooshing them into her teeth.

"*Please remember the accident,*" he whispered into her ear.

She stopped, leaning against him.

He slowly let her mouth go, grabbing her shoulder and gently turning her around. "You're Bethany." He smiled.

She shook her head, furrowing her brow. Her head hurt, and she thought it was more than a tension headache.

17

"And I'm Neil," he paused, a gleam in his eye that gave her a sick feeling, "your husband."

She sobbed, startling herself and the man she didn't know. "No," she said.

Neil shook his head, his smile spread too wide across his face. "Honey, what do you mean no?" He reached to touch her face, and she smacked it away. "I hope your memory comes back soon." His head bowed, and he sulked back to the dinner table.

Charlotte stared at a photo he had been standing in front of.

A picturesque, lily-covered archway towered above a couple embracing, the woman in a long white gown, the man—

She gasped.

"Bathroom?" she asked, flinging her hands out as if she was disgusted with what was on them.

He quickly stood up, guiding her down the hall. He flicked the light on.

She felt a deep nausea build in the pit of her stomach until bile splattered the tile at her feet.

He gasped, some of the orange fluid on his socks.

She stared at herself, lips gleaming. Her bobbed, brown hair was brushed back, with two pink clips holding it away from her face, just like the woman in the photo. It felt gross. She didn't know why; she didn't know herself from anything.

"What happened to me?" she asked, her voice soft. Her wide eyes roamed over the gentle blue plaid dress she wore. It fit her body well but made her queasy. It didn't *feel* like hers. Looking back to Neil, she waited for an answer as the back of her head throbbed with each pulse of her heart.

Lightly setting his hand on her shoulder, he said, "You fell off a horse, and it *trampled you*."

Chills shot up her spine as all the pain in her body made sense. Tears sprouted free, smearing her heavy mascara.

She didn't remember the bathtub three feet behind her. She didn't remember spending a comatose week there. She didn't remember the bottles of pills she had carefully been fed or the life that had slowly slipped from her mind.

Charlotte was gone.

Is this really my home? Is this strange man really my husband? Have I really forgotten the life we've made together?

Dinner was bland, yet Neil smiled through the entire thing. His eyes trailed every move she made as she picked at her plate.

She abruptly set her fork down. "What's my name again?"

"Bethany Ridges." It rolled out of his mouth so naturally that it must've been her name. "You were Bethany Free before we got married."

She smiled, a dimple appearing on her left cheek, and his eyes flicked to a large photo on the wall beside her. A brown-haired woman with a bob cut smiled in the photo, a dimple on her right cheek.

He cleared his throat, averting his eyes from the photo. "Everyone joked about that when I proposed."

"About what?" Her brown eyes widened, her curiosity piqued. She held her fork midway to her mouth, a pea plopping into the soggy meat.

"About your last name. *Free.*" He chuckled, crow's feet deeply creasing beside his eyes. Despite his cheery manner, this disturbed Charlotte. "*Well, she isn't Free now!*" he blurted in a high-pitched voice that drilled her ears. She flinched, a sharp pain streaking across the back of her head. He laughed loudly, yet his eyes remained fixed on Charlotte, never fully alighting as his smile did. Sweat broke out across his brow as his cackles climbed higher and higher, sending nails into the back of her head.

A wave of nausea carried her to the bathroom, where bile and a handful of peas splashed into the water. She watched what looked like melted plastic float on the surface of her bile.

He quickly followed behind and patted her back lightly, cooing to her. "Oh, those pain pills must really be affecting your appetite."

His wavering voice trailed ice in her veins. She pulled away from him, leaning her back against the bathtub as she landed on the floor with a huff. Looking up to him, she dry heaved.

"I think you should rest." He offered his hand.

With hesitation, she took it.

Lightheaded, she followed him to the back of the house, where the bedroom resided. As he opened the door, Charlotte locked up.

Pure-white walls surrounded a tan carpeted room entirely furnished with white- and cream-colored woods and surfaces. Restraints dangled from the bed posts.

"*No*," she whispered, pulling away from him as he dragged her in. Her socked feet slid on the carpet below her, heating up as she struggled.

"Bethany, please, just rest," he said, grabbing her free arm with his other hand.

Her fist shot out, hitting him in the eye. She cried, running down the hall. Again, the front door called to her as she tore through the living room. She reached for the handle, noticing a smear of makeup on her hand.

He grabbed her from behind, yelling in her ear.

A restless feeling, like a bundle of coiled wire trying to escape her gut, filled her. She flailed in his arms, wishing he would let her go.

Her elbows found his ribs, striking over and over again. He picked her up, slipping on the tile before the front door. Instead of taking the fall and protecting the one whom he called *wife*, Neil twisted and thrusted his weight onto her, smashing her head into the tile.

Five

Charlotte opened her eyes to take in a giant head. It stared at her, its wide eyes menacing. The edges of her vision were fuzzy.

A thunderous roar came from within this head as it opened and closed its maw with fervor. It reared back into darkness as if sucked up by a huge vacuum. Seconds later, it returned, a giant hand brushing something cold and scratchy across her forehead. Water dripped into her eye, stinging it enough to make her hiss.

"I'm so glad you're awake!"

She found clarity as her senses woke slower than her mind.

"Now we can drink some tea together." Neil smiled, flashing his nasty teeth at her.

A bitter taste filled her mouth as she thought of warm tea. "I don't like tea," she croaked as he stood up from crouching beside her at the couch.

He abruptly spun around, brow furrowed. "Of course you do, *Bethany*. We drink tea every evening."

She shook her head and spoke slowly, "I may not remember myself or you, but I do remember that tea tastes like dirty leaf water." She found herself amused by the statement, and a smile spread across her lips, quickly diffused by the look on his face.

"We'll see about that."

The chairs at the kitchen bar were stiff and uncomfortable, the wear marks in the wrong place for her butt.

"That's not your seat," he said, pouring steaming water into a mug laced with dried leaves.

She looked down at the weathered, dark leather between her thighs. "Well, where do I sit?"

"On the left side, so we don't bump elbows." He carried her mug over to the sink, grabbing a pill bottle hidden behind the sugar canister. Pulling out three pills, he popped them each open and dumped the powder into the quickly browning water. On the side of the bottle read the name of a woman long since deceased. Her prescriptions were often filled nonetheless and stored in Neil's pantry. Just on the other side of the bottle read, *Warning. May cause excessive vomiting, short term memory loss, and/or suicidal thoughts.*

"Bump elbows?"

He slammed another mug onto the counter, his lips pulled up at the corners. "Yes, Bethany. You're left-handed, I'm right-handed." He pulled out a spoon, opened the sugar canister, and stirred in some sugar. *Bitter leaf water,* he scoffed in his head.

Charlotte looked down at her left hand, her eyes glancing over the small, plain wedding band and charm bracelet around her wrist. Noticing engraving, she pulled her wrist closer and inspected it. *Bethany* read one of the silver charms.

He set her mug in front of her, and little did it surprise her that it read *Bethany* in black cursive. She reached for it, but he quickly slapped her hand away.

Her eyes snapped up to him, her brow furrowed.

"You're *left-handed*," he spat, holding his hand up at her.

She reached forward with her left hand, gripping the hot ceramic. Picking it up felt odd, but she successfully took a sip under his watchful eye.

He slipped onto the stool next to her, dangling his feet like a child.

A word came to her mind, and she smiled. "Do you have any root beer?"

His face scrunched. "Root beer?"

"Yeah, I like root beer."

He shook his head. "No, you don't."

She stared down at her tea, focus hardening her face. She looked back to his disgruntled countenance. "Isn't that the word?" she asked softly, her eyes hinting at sadness.

"Root beer is nasty carbonated sugar."

"It's brown, isn't it?"

"It is."

"Yeah, yeah, I like root beer. It's sweet, and, and…tingly!" She smiled, the first inkling of herself returning.

"*No!*" He slammed his fist onto the counter. "We don't drink soda or alcohol in this house."

Charlotte cowered away from him, tempted to make a run for the door.

"Beth, I'm sorry."

She flinched when his hand landed on her shoulder.

"I just want you to remember *yourself*." He stared deep into her eyes, angered at the tinge of blue around the irises that wasn't supposed to be there. "I miss you."

Sending a spear into his heart, she said, "I just don't know you. I don't even know who I am." She put her hands out, palms up, gesturing at the room. "I don't even know where I am."

His face slackened. From tight lips, he said, "You look tired. Want to watch a movie?"

She almost shook her head, wanting to go outside instead. The hard look in his eyes made her nod *yes*.

They moved into the living room after making popcorn. Before the opening credits had even ended, Neil tried to put his arm around her shoulders. She skirted his advances by flopping onto the floor and saying, "The couch is too lumpy."

He looked down at her, displeased.

Thirty minutes of agony passed before he passed out. Charlotte may not have known her name, but she was sure she didn't like romantic comedies.

Holding her breath, she stood up and tiptoed away from the couch. The front door called to her as it had many times before. She pulled on the handle, noticing it was locked. When she reached to twist the knob, her fingers grazed a keyhole.

That's not normal, is it? There's supposed to be a swivel thing here, right?

She backed away from the door on light feet. Neil's snores floated to her ears from the couch. She sped by him, hoping to find the back door.

Through the kitchen she'd only been in twice since regaining consciousness, she found another room—a small, tiled room with a half-sized table. There was a large space where she assumed a glass door had been, but instead of transparent glass looking out to the place she was, plywood boarded up over a partially broken glass door. Brown dribbles dirtied the crystalline shards still littering the cream tile.

Finally approaching desperation, she ran up to a window, where she discovered brackets screwed from the windowsill into the frame of the window with a padlock. The shutters outside the glass were closed, blocking any view of the outside world.

This isn't right. This isn't normal.

Through the kitchen and down the hall, she went into the bedroom Neil insisted she had been sharing with him. Each window was the same, even the small one high in the bathroom wall. She opened a door she didn't recognize only to find hanging clothes.

There has to be a key somewhere.

She pushed aside the clothing, seeing a seam in the wall. Her heart raced as she pushed on it, hopeful to find an escape. As it inched open, a faint blue glow filled the closet. She ducked into the room, saddened by its closed walls. A small desk held a computer that was displaying its homepage: a photo of Neil and the woman named Bethany on their wedding day. She felt no attachment to the picture.

The walls around her were coated in taped photographs and posters. As she looked closer, a wave of nausea struck her. Naked women in all positions stared back at her, some willingly, some seeming unaware a camera was present, and some clearly under the influence.

She averted her eyes, looking toward the computer, where different photos took up the wall space—photos of her with her brown bob cut and generally comely clothing, and photos of a young blonde girl, her face strikingly like her own. The blonde girl clearly didn't know the photos were being taken, as they were many times taken from behind something or through glass. A screenshot of a social profile sat next to the computer on the desk. It was the blonde girl. Her name was Charlotte Brenegan. The name sent a chill down her spine.

What if I'm not Bethany? Fear and rage filled Charlotte's mind. *Who is this blonde girl?*

A voice from a deeper part of her mind whispered, *Who am I?*

She huffed. *If I'm Neil's wife, why does he have all this?*

She pushed to remember anything about herself or her life, only bringing up a feeling of anger toward the man that was supposed to be her husband.

She stormed out of the hidden room, her bobbed hair swinging back and forth as she made her way to the living room. Standing over Neil's loose, wrinkled face, she pulled her arm back. She swung down hard, the meat of her palm striking the side of his face.

He woke violently, falling off the couch onto the carpet below. His bowl of popcorn spewed buttery puffs across the floor. Without a word, he stood and grabbed her by the shoulders, shaking her.

She held her composure, asking, "What is that hidden room in our closet?"

His face went from red with anger to unsure to suddenly calm. "Well, you weren't supposed to find that." His voice was even.

"No shit, Neil. If I'm your wife, why do you have all that? Who are all those women?! *Who's Charlotte?!*" Her voice raised to a shriek.

He let her go. "You need to take your medication."

"What medication?"

"It's for pain, since your accident."

"I'm not in pain. I'm angry."

"Well, you have to take it anyway."

"No."

"Damn it, Bethany." Neil threw himself at her, locking his arm around her neck. He applied vigorous pressure as she writhed.

This moment sparked another chill down her spine even as she struggled for air. It was all remarkably familiar, and the image of a corn field flashed across her mind.

He held tight until she went limp in his arms. He dropped her, letting her slump to the floor.

Walking into the kitchen, Neil sighed. From a cabinet above the sink, he retrieved a sterile syringe, and from a box in the fridge, he grabbed a small bottle with a foil top. Stabbing the top with the syringe, he sucked up the contents then pushed out the air.

Charlotte, still sprawled out on the floor, breathed softly. He took her wrist and rotated her arm so he could see the inside. A little blue vein protruded from inside her elbow. He penetrated this with the needle and plunged it.

She wouldn't remember that room tomorrow.

"College-age Californian girl may be miss—"

"You're awake!" Neil sprang from his seat in the cushy recliner that resided in the corner of the living room.

Charlotte's head hung over the couch cushion, her neck sore. Feeling like she had a ball of cotton stuffed into her mouth, she sat up, pulling away from him.

"How are you feeling?"

"Sore. Why did I fall asleep like that?"

"Fall a—yeah, you fell asleep during the movie."

"Must have been boring." Her neck throbbed in unison with her skull. She couldn't remember anything but tea and spilled popcorn.

He slid onto the couch next to her, wrapping his arm around her. She squirmed as he pulled her closer. "I've enjoyed this time together."

She sighed, letting him squish her. She still had an urge. "When can I go outside?"

"Maybe soon. The doctor said bright light can give you headaches."

"I don't remember my doctor." Her shoulders drooped.

He squeezed her tighter. "That's okay. She's kinda a bitch."

Charlotte snapped him a look from the corner of her eye, irked at the use of his language. The word seemed foreign in his mouth, like a schoolteacher repeating the bad word a child used to their parents.

"I'm sorry, I know you don't like swearing."

She seized this opportunity to shrug him off. "It's fine." She stood up, parading into the kitchen as he followed at her heels.

Besides her sore neck, she felt no pain. Only brief blips of the last few days filled her mind, and while she wasn't at ease, she thought she might be on the road to recovery. She didn't notice the limp in her stride or the steady bleeding of the back of her head. Her stomach churned nauseatingly, and unbeknownst to her, another capsule bled through its casing, filling her bloodstream with a steady flow of mind-numbing chemicals.

His body heat radiated onto her back and the left side of her neck as she stared into the fridge.

She could live with him for now, as he cared for her in her illness, but she knew the instant she got better she would leave him. His touch felt like cactus needles brushing her skin. She opened her mouth, nasty words rising through her throat, when the doorbell rang.

"I'll get it!" He rushed out.

She slammed the fridge shut, her curiosity piqued. *An outsider.* On tiptoes, she peered around the entranceway to the kitchen, seeing a man at their door.

"Nice to see you, Laurence! What's shakin'?"

The officer glared down at him, his lips puckered in mild disgust. His demeanor cracked, revealing a bright smile.

Charlotte narrowed her eyes on this stranger.

"Good morning, Neil." His voice boomed through the house. He spoke louder than anyone she had ever heard, to her recollection. "Can I come in?" the man asked, hands on his wide hips.

Neil hesitated, staring up at the burly man. His scrawny figure cowered before the officer as he stepped aside.

Laurence came in, wiping his shoes as Neil gently closed the door. Facing away from Neil, the smile fell from Laurence's face. He seemed nervous.

Why is he allowed in, but I'm not allowed out?

Laurence looked up, his weary eyes meeting hers. His smile returned, more genuine this time. "Bethany, how are you?"

The name was still foreign to her, and she held back a cringe as she slinked around the entranceway. She kicked herself for not getting a peek outside. As he stared at her, hundreds of words crossed her mind, all ranging from *terrified* to *furious*. She allowed herself a smile to match his, and said, "I'm alright."

The officer's face changed. His smile dropped, concern taking its place.

Neil quickly jumped in, setting a light hand on the man's shoulder. "Beth had an accident."

"An accident?" His eyes never left hers. The concern on his face grew.

"Yes." Neil paused, seeming to wipe a tear from his eye. "She fell off her horse this last weekend. Doctor says she has amnesia."

She glanced down at the officer's uniform, reading his name tag, L. Brenegan. Chills shot down her spine as tears sprinkled into her eyes. "Brenegan," she whispered, the chill shooting up her spine a second time.

"What was that?" Neil asked.

"Brenegan." Her eyes lost focus as she felt a deep connection to the name.

"Yes, this is Officer Brenegan," Neil said, talking slowly and over pronouncing each word.

"Do you remember me?" Brenegan asked.

"No," she said sharply.

Brenegan nodded and looked down at Neil from the corner of his eye. "Well, I came here today to discuss someone with the same last name."

Neil's eyes widened.

"Will you please excuse us?" Laurence asked her.

She felt a pang in her chest, frustrated he would ask her to excuse them when this was supposed to be her house. She sank back into the kitchen.

Again, she stood at the open fridge, blankly staring at a block of cheese. When the front door closed and silence encased the house, she crept into the living room. Her desperation for the outside was broken when she heard their conversation. Without hesitation, she leaned her ear against the crack of the door.

"—id you say her name was?" Neil asked.

Why is he talking so fast?

"Charlotte Brenegan."

A deep feeling of familiarity struck her, sending a tsunami of emotion over her. Sorrow, fury, nostalgia, and confusion washed through her. It took everything in her to get herself to concentrate on the conversation once again.

"Were you gone from April 7th through April 15th?"

Her heart thudded in her ears as she waited for an answer.

"Yes."

"Why were you gone?"

"I was visiting my brother."

"Where was Bethany?"

"Here."

There was a pause.

"Why are you asking me all this?"

"There's a missing woman in California. Your travel time matches up with the time she was abducted. I don't see you as that sort of person, but it's protocol to ask anyone that could be involved."

"Why would I be involved?" Neil asked, his voice cracking at the end of his question.

"A man of your description was seen in town."

Another pause. Her heart pumped heavy in her ears.

"A man of your description was seen with a girl witnesses believe to be Charlotte." There was a pause, and the officer laughed lightly, as if they were at a barbeque and not discussing Neil's potential involvement in the kidnapping of a young woman. "Although, they did say he had hair, and Neil, you haven't had any since '98."

Neil forcefully laughed.

The officer's voice was suddenly harsh. "Some say they believe it was a wig. Others say the man was bald."

"I was with my brother the *entire* trip," Neil snapped.

"I believe you, Neil. I just gotta let you know that if this girl doesn't come up within the next few days, you're gonna be under the microscope." He sighed. "You better have an alibi. This story is huge, and *everyone* is on the lookout. The guy took her in broad daylight and was seen driving with her in the passenger seat. There's photo evidence from multiple stop lights. I can't stop them from looking in your direction."

"Why am I even a suspect?" Neil asked, the desperation clear as crystal.

"Your credit card was used at a gas station in the last town she was spotted."

The silence was thick. Charlotte's breath heaved out of her forcefully. Her stomach sank.

"This case is from *California,* and they're thinking *I'm* involved?" Neil asked.

"Last place they were spotted was two counties over."

She so desperately wanted to believe she really was Bethany. She wanted to believe the wound on the back of her head was from the hoof of a horse and not foul play. She wanted to believe the only person she knew in this world was telling the truth.

But she had a feeling he wasn't.

"I—I picked up a junkie. She needed a ride to a few towns over that I was crossing through." Neil's voice was soft and hurt. "She reminded me of my sister, bless her soul. But she bounced on me at a gas station." He sniveled. "I just wanted to talk some sense into her."

Is he really that sad about it? Charlotte wondered.

"You're a good man, Neil. I'm sure this will all blow over, and they'll find the guy that really kidnapped this woman, despite him looking a lot like you." Laurence laughed again.

Charlotte froze, sure the door was going to open into the side of her face as she listened to Brenegan crunch through the gravel away from the door.

"Ah!"

She glued herself back onto the doorframe.

"Gonna be planting a big garden?"

She walked to the window beside the door, tempted to rip the screwed-in blinds from their place. She wedged her finger between the window frame and the stiff blinds, pulling toward herself until a spot of light came through. Putting her face close, she could peer through this small hole. Her eyes landed on Laurence, who stood on a gravel driveway. That was all she could see, and when he made eye contact with her, she jerked back, letting the blinds snap back in place.

"Yep! I'll make sure to send over all the extra tomatoes. I know how much Clara likes them!"

She scurried into the kitchen, snatched up a loaf of bread, and pretended to be putting together a sandwich.

Neil came in shortly after, a scowl on his face.

She turned away from him, cutting up an onion.

"I can't believe the accident has affected you so badly."

She looked at him from the corner of her eye, seeing he had his face buried in his hands.

"Laurence is very concerned for you." A short lapse of silence fell over them. "He asked why you were talking strange."

"Talking strange?" she asked, slathering the bread in mayonnaise.

"Since when do you eat sandwiches like that?" he asked, his voice raised.

She cowered at his tone. "I don't—"

He snatched up the plate and tossed it in the trash. "You like salads and rice and light things. It's how you keep your figure."

Her stomach growled.

"And you've been talking *all wrong!*"

"Wrong?" her voice wavered.

"Yes!" He snapped. "Where did your Southern Georgian accent go?" He approached her, grabbing a fistful of hair from the back of her head. She felt a flare of heat and pain from under his fingers. His weathered eyes bore into hers. "You'd better start talking right."

She nodded, her scalp hurting.

"*Repeat. After. Me.*" He took a deep breath, lessening his grip on her hair. "Sally grows tomatoes vastly in her garden." His high-pitched, southern drawl gave her a smirk, which he tightened his grip for. "*Say it.*"

"Sally grows tomatoes in her garden."

"*Vastly.*"

"Vastly?"

"*Sally grows tomatoes vastly in her garden.*"

Tears rose in her eyes as she was sure the back of her head was going to be bald. "Sally grows tomatoes vastly in her garden," she repeated with her best southern accent.

"Tah-maw-toes," he said through clenched teeth.

"Tomatoes."

"*Tah-maw-toes!*" He yelled.

Charlotte took a deep breath and said slowly, "Tah-maw-toes."

Neil's scrunched face relaxed into a smile. His hand retreated from her hair and touched her cheek. "That's more like it, Bethany." His eyes fell into the trash, then jumped back to her. "How'd you like to go to the store?"

Her eyes widened, and she nodded.

Six

I don't remember any of this.

After a quick wipe down with a washcloth, the shower having given her the heebie-jeebies, Charlotte dressed herself in a flannel and jeans. The cowgirl boots Neil provided were too snug on her pinky toe, rubbing it uncomfortably raw, but he insisted she wear her favorite pair of shoes.

The day was clear and warm, and she drank in all the sights. She spotted the fresh plot of dirt Laurence spoke of, which lay just in front of an old, rickety toolshed. It was about ten feet long and 3 feet wide. Something about it made her nauseous.

Her stomach dropped further when she saw his car. A bad feeling, like a dark aura, clung to it, especially emanating from the interior. She bit her tongue as she slipped into the passenger seat. The vinyl seat cradled her crawling skin.

Empty fields surrounded the small house for what looked to be miles. She knew she wouldn't have a chance of escaping this place alive.

Curiosity kept her complacent. So far, two people insisted she was *Bethany*, both Neil and Laurence, and she supposed being Bethany was better than being the nobody she remembered or, rather, the person she forgot.

She buckled herself in as he slid into the driver's seat.

"Glad to see you didn't forget *everything*," he said, starting the car.

His tone stung her. She wanted to talk back just as snarkily but didn't want to have to go through the charade of her unfamiliar southern accent. It was more work than she thought her normal voice ought to have been.

The drive was quiet as he refused to turn the radio on. He said Bethany didn't like music.

"Hmm?" Charlotte replied, certain he was wrong. Silence was okay, but she felt like she was going crazy as the AC buzzed around something in the vent.

Vzzz. Vzzzzz. VZZZZZ.

"You'd better behave in the store," he said. He gripped the wheel with a tight hand.

"Why wouldn't I behave?" she asked, faking the southern drawl. Images of her running away from him flashed through her mind.

He braked suddenly, almost sending her into the dash, then whipped around a corner, pulling into the parking lot of a large store.

"No reason."

The store was busy, and Charlotte saw the most people she'd ever seen, to her recollection. They bustled around cars, shoving carts this way and that. Cars fought for parking spaces, angry drivers honked and yelled out windows. Her heart raced in her chest.

They got out of the car as soon as Neil found a parking space, and she fantasized about running away. She could feel her squished toes aching to pound the asphalt. She would run until her lungs exploded if she could just get a second away.

Where would I go? Who would I be? Well, I could be anybo—

He snatched her hand as she stared out at the busy street. "Let's get a move on, Ms. Space Cadet," he said, facing away from her. She could hear how he said it through gritted teeth. His grip hurt her hand, but she feared protesting would cause a scene.

As they walked into the store with a crowd of people, she couldn't help but feel helpless. Who was she to question him? But who was he to tell her who she was?

"Shredded or grated parmesan?" Neil asked.

Charlotte's wide eyes scanned the cheese aisle. Bright colors swirled around her, packages screaming *Pick me! Buy me!*

35

"Bethany."

She snapped her attention to him. "Yes?"

"Grated or shredded parmesan?" His jaw tensed.

"Uh—whichever you like. I'm not particular to either." Her southern accent sailed smoothly out of her red lips. He had insisted she paint them before going out.

He smiled. "Alright."

"Bethany!" a shrill voice called from the end of the aisle. They had gone through three-quarters of the store without being noticed.

She spun around, her chest bound with barbed wire.

A woman with a head full of wild, blonde ringlets quickly approached, setting her handheld basket down to hug Charlotte. "How are you?" she asked, holding Charlotte by the shoulders.

Neil placed his hand on Charlotte's lower back. "Do you remember Ramona?"

The woman glanced at him, her smile slowly pulled down. "Wh—what's wrong?"

He sighed. "Bethany was in an accident."

"*An accident?*" She grabbed Charlotte by the face, a clammy hand on each cheek. Looking deep into her eyes, she asked, "Are you okay?"

Charlotte was torn between nodding and shaking her head.

"She just has amnesia from a bump on the head. The doc says it could be permanent, but it's more than likely to be temporary. I just gotta keep jogging her memory." He gave a light smile.

Ramona returned it, looking back into Charlotte's eyes. "Well, I'm Ramona Griffin. I was your neighbor until you and Neil moved to the house on Anchor Lane."

Charlotte nodded, no recollection of this clingy woman. Her breath reeked of coffee, and she stood too close for Charlotte to escape it.

Ramona's eyes glanced over to her thumb, which resided on a birthmark she had never seen on Bethany's face before. "What happened?"

"She fell off her horse while I was out of state visiting my brother. It's a good thing I had already been on my way home. I can't imagine anyone would have seen her lying on the ground by our shed from the road."

"Goodness! How long was she lying out there?"

"I'm not sure. She was unconscious when I found her." He kissed Charlotte on the cheek.

She tried to keep the repulsion from spilling out onto her face, catching a curious look from Ramona.

"Well," she paused, "I better get going. Bill is waiting on me." She chuckled. "Can't have a hungry man waitin' too long." Passing the couple, she gave a small wave. "Toodles! Hope you start to remember yourself soon, Bethany."

Charlotte watched her scurry down the aisle and disappear, feeling a strange sense of longing.

Neil returned to hunting cheeses as Charlotte stared at passing shoppers.

I could know any of these people.

Although she thought it, she didn't feel it. The only familiar face around her was Neil, and even he had his alien parts about him. She wanted to slip away, fall into the sea of faces, never to be noticed again. She took a step, parting herself from the cart.

His hand wrenched onto her arm. "We're going this way, sweetheart." He sighed, slipping an arm around her shoulders as she pushed the cart. "I do wish you'd remember yourself."

The song playing over the speakers reminded her of something. She dared not mention it to him as the unsavory feeling of not quite grasping a memory took her focus. Staring at the floor with intense concentration on her face, she bumped into a young man in a leather jacket.

They both gasped, eyes meeting.

"Hey—"

"I'm so sorry," she said, pulling her basket away. The insignia on his shirt caught her eye. She glanced down and read, "Good Charlotte." Chills shot up her spine, and as the familiar song reached its climax, she remembered her first prom.

The young man had already scurried off as she stood motionless, an expression of utter shock on her face.

A hand landed on the back of her neck. Cold and rough, it squeezed tightly until she turned around.

Neil's smiling face met hers, so covered in wrinkles and sunspots.

"How old am I?" she asked.

His face contorted as if he'd stuck a lemon wedge in his mouth. "You're twenty-nine, Bethany."

She listened to the song just as it ended, the memory of her dancing with a young man playing in the background of her mind. The boy had no face as she couldn't recall it, and they danced in a sea of purples and blues as she couldn't figure out the setting. "When did this song come out?"

Neil shook his head. "Listen, Beth, we gotta get going. I need to start on dinner since you can't seem to remember any recipes." He hooked his arm through hers and took control of the cart, sailing them toward the self-checkout.

The drive home was dipped in silence as she stared out the window. *I don't feel twenty-nine, and, well...I don't feel like Bethany, either.*

Glancing out of the corner of her eye, she could see how physically upset Neil appeared. He was tense. His hands gripped the wheel tightly as if he wanted to strangle the life out of it.

The entire time she had been conscious, she knew she was afraid, but for the first time, she admitted to herself, *I'm scared. And I'm certainly not Bethany.*

"Get the groceries out of the trunk. I'll get them out of the backseat," Neil said, parking the car.

Thin rain clouds moved in, making the warm day muggy. As small drops plipped onto the gravel road, Charlotte envisioned herself running. The road up to their house was long and lonely. The only homes on their street were all abandoned, and the nearest used road was the freeway. Acres of forest separated them from the moving cars, and she didn't think she could get out from under his view with enough time to make it.

"*Bethany!*"

She jumped, turning to face the house.

Neil stood in the doorway, his figure seeming to take up the whole entrance. "You gonna bring in them bags or just stand in the rain?"

She realized the sky was pouring warm, fat droplets onto her, splashing the white plastic bags in the trunk. Grabbing a bag, she spotted a ruddy stain in the gray carpet. *Wine or blood?*

She scurried into the house, the thought sparking new ideas about him. Setting the bags on the counter, she caught him pacing, a hand on his chin, fingers splayed across his tight lips. She tried to rush back outside to grab the rest of the bags.

"You really pissed me off out there," he blurted as she reached the front door.

She stepped outside, and for the first time, she was sure of herself as she sped down the driveway. Her feet smashed on the gravel, and the line of trees called to her, their dull green her safe haven. She could imagine herself living in the forest until the forest lived in her. The cycle continued.

A hard crack, and she crumpled to the ground, her body crimson with cider. Dark-green glass protruded from her twinkling scalp and glittered from the jagged rock around her.

Neil stood over her, panting, his juice splattered lips pulled back in a snarl.

He dragged her into the house, careful to lay a towel beneath her. She slid nicely along the tiled floor just until he stuffed her into the bathroom. He muttered to himself as he loaded the rest of the groceries into the house.

"*She's Bethany. She's Bethany, and she's alive. And alive Bethany loves me. And dead Bethany …*" His eyes glanced over at the fresh plot in the garden. "Bethany's not dead, she's on the bathroom floor. She needs more pills. More pills, and she'll be more Bethany."

With trembling hands, he grabbed every bottle of pills he had and a bottle of vodka from the very back of the fridge, something he knew the old Bethany had been hiding from him. The pill bottles in his hands all shared the same name. *Rebecca Joy* had been kept on antidepressants, anxiety meds, and blood thinners until her heart exploded one day, but only one man at the pharmacy knew that. Behind the counter where he worked, he kept her prescriptions more alive than her body ever would be. He rushed into the bathroom and kneeled by Charlotte's side. He opened the bottles and poured out two pills, one at a time, until he held a handful of colors. One by one, he placed them on her tongue and drowned them in vodka. Her eyes fluttered but did not open as she struggled to swallow. They seemed to be going down.

He yearned to hold Bethany again as he poured the last of the vodka down Charlotte's throat. He left her on the bathroom floor to put the groceries away, and when that was done, he checked on her. "Bethany?" he asked, peering around the bathroom door.

Charlotte lay like a ragdoll in front of the bathtub, her skin and clothing stained red. Her chest was still, and no breath could be heard from her gaping mouth.

Fear pierced his chest. He got down on his knees next to her and put his ear to her lips.

Nothing.

He put two fingers on her neck, waited, then moved them to her wrist.

Nothing.

"Oh," Neil stood up, "oh, my God." He ran out of the bathroom and down the hall, where he stopped at a closet. Throwing open the door, he tossed aside a jacket here and a box there until he held a small plastic case. He ran to her side once more, unzipping the defibrillator and pulling out two patches. Being a pharmacist, he wasn't entirely sure how it worked. He had seen it used once at work, on an old man. It had restarted his heart, and he hoped it would do the same for his Bethany.

The buttons frightened him. He wasn't sure what to do. Clearing his mind, he saw the power button and punched it. The machine beeped and the screen lit up. He ripped open her flannel and stuck the two patches on her collarbone and ribs, just as the diagram showed.

Seconds passed as the machine scanned her.

Neil waited impatiently.

She convulsed, air rushing from her lips. He smiled, and she jumped again. The machine beeped with her heart rate. He ripped the pads from her chest and checked her pulse himself. It was light, but it was there.

I've resurrected her.

"Bethany, Bethany, wake up!" He patted her face, a smile pulling on his lips, but she wouldn't open her eyes. "You're supposed to wake up now. I fixed your heart."

She lay still, her heart only faintly beating in her chest.

"No." Tears rolled down his cheeks. He grabbed her under her armpits and picked her up, propping her up against the bathtub. "No, not another one." Bathroom cabinets flew open as he searched. He tossed aside old prescriptions and soaps. Gasping, he found it—a little bottle of nasal spray. He crawled over to her almost-lifeless body and shoved the neck of the bottle up her left nostril. Neil pressed down on it, spraying what he hoped would save her into her sinuses.

Seven

*Fiery pain. Everything. Pain. Pain. **Pain.***

Bethany's eyes sprang open as she gasped for air. Neil's ugly face stared at her, his eyes bloodshot and a weak smile on his face. She reared back and smacked him. He grabbed his cheek. The expression of hurt on his face pleased Bethany. She tried to stand, to be above him, but found she couldn't. Instead, she sat and reveled in his tears.

He lunged at her, hugging her fiercely. They remained that way as she wondered why she couldn't remember yesterday or any time before that. Afraid to alert her husband, she sat in silence.

He finally let go and helped her to her feet. He guided her into the shower and left her to attend to herself.

When the door clicked closed, she cringed and hopped out of the shower. Something in there wasn't right.

The back of her head throbbed. She touched the bloody welt at the base of her skull and winced. The bathroom was a mess. She grabbed a washcloth from the pill-bottle littered floor, and wetting it under warm water, she wiped away the red stains.

She looked in the mirror at herself, finally feeling at home in her body. Her eyes narrowed.

I hate that man. I know damn well he's responsible.

She shook out the glass still stuck in her short hair and rinsed out what juice she could get with the sink's weak water pressure. As she dried her hair, she wondered why she was still married to him if she hated him so much. Her eyes trailed over the red-splotched bra she wore. She slipped it off and sniffed it. Rather than the metallic tang of blood that she expected, she got a whiff of sweet fruit. She wondered why she was stuck in this horrible house. If only she could remember something besides the fact that she was married to him and that she had a hankering for tea.

Skin red from vigorously scrubbing, Bethany threw on the sweatpants and T-shirt that had been neatly folded and placed onto the counter. She swung the door open, meeting a wide-eyed Neil, whose hand was up, braced to knock on the door.

He opened his mouth to speak, the doorbell taking the place of his words. As he rushed off to answer it, she stormed off into the kitchen, hopeful to find a salad. She was starving.

A woman's voice perked her ear, and she found herself listening to the conversation. *It's that hag from the store.* She shook her head, dousing the lettuce in ranch.

Store?

Foggy memories of a trip to the supermarket sprang to the forefront of her attention. Images of Ramona, horse teeth in a wide smile and the smell of rank coffee, overwhelmed her.

"Neil, I need to talk to you." Ramona's voice was stern, barely audible all the way in the kitchen.

Bethany tiptoed to the archway that separated the kitchen from the living room.

"What is it, Ramona?"

"I think it's awful strange a young girl goes missing the week you're outta town and now your wife's missing a few wrinkles."

Bethany's fist clenched.

"What are you saying?" he asked, his voice strained and high.

"What did you do to Bethany? Where is she?!" The old woman's voice cracked as she hollered. Bethany could hear the tears in her words. "I know you picked up a lil hussy junkie! And I know you dolled her up to look like Bethany!"

"God dammit, woman, what is your problem?" Bethany slid out into the room, her chin held high.

Ramona staggered back away from the doorway at the sight, but she slung a finger toward her. "You hussy! Where is Bethany?!" she screeched.

"You dumb, old woman. You got Alzheimer's? Dementia? Can't ya see me right in front of your face?"

Neil watched in awe as Bethany's southern drawl slid out smoother than molasses.

"Where is she?" Ramona bared her teeth at Bethany, her eyes wild.

"Ma'am, I suggest you leave before I hog tie you and roast you like the pig you are." Bethany folded her arms across her chest.

An astonished grin spread across his face. *I've resurrected her.*

Ramona reached into her purse, slipping out a revolver. She pointed it at Bethany, her extended hand trembling. Before either could speak, Neil tackled the old woman, sending the gun across the floor. He landed on top of her, sure to press a heavy hand against her forehead as they sailed through the air. She wailed until her head met the concrete porch, a sigh cutting her off as she lay limp. He scrambled to his feet, looking for the pistol.

Bethany scooped up the gun, pulled back the hammer, and fired into the old woman's chest three times. Her body jolted with each bullet, sending a spray of blood out of her lips. A split second passed before Bethany aimed again and fired twice into Ramona's head, splattering crimson brain matter across their front porch.

"Bethany." Neil looked over at her, catching sight of the revolver's barrel. He stared into the black hole.

She smiled, her eyes dark. "One more in the chamber, Neil."

"Be—"

The gun swiveled, firing one last bullet into Ramona's stomach.

"We're going to bury her in the new garden, Neil." She tossed the gun, and it bounced off Ramona's face and onto the ground.

Neil stared at the body as Bethany grabbed her salad from the kitchen. She sat on the couch, crossing her legs as the smell of shit entered the open doorway.

Flies buzzed around them as they dug up fresh earth. The sun beat down on Neil's sweating back, and Bethany stood watching, on break. She strutted to the open door of the shed and glanced over at his butt as he bent over to wipe dirt from his shiny shoe.

Boot covered in mud, she planted her foot on the seat of his tan pants and shoved. A wry smile twisted her lips as he fell.

Having been holding the shovel with one hand and smearing dirt off his shoe with the other, he took the mud face-first. On his hands and knees, he gagged, mud spilling from his mouth.

She laughed. "*Oink. Oink. Oink.*"

He blushed as he stood up, spitting gritty saliva onto Ramona's body.

"Neil, what day is it?" she asked.

"Tuesday. Why?"

"No, what's the date?"

"What day do you think it is?"

"I—" She paused. "I don't know."

"It's April 18th. What's got you worried, Beth?"

She hesitated, staring out at the tree line. "I'm not worried. Just couldn't think of it off the top of my head."

"You've always loved this time of year."

She looked back to him, pushing down the smile that arose at the sight of him covered in mud. "Because?"

"Because the light rain and the garden." He gently smiled, mud slipping down his face. "I actually made this plot bigger for you before I went to see my brother. I'm sorry you can't remember."

"It is what it is, Neil." She sighed, walking around him and digging her shovel into the mud next to Ramona's mangled head. "Go wash up. I'll finish out here."

He walked off without a word, hosing off with the hose out front, then trampling to the backdoor as she shoveled.

With each shovel full, she felt more weight press on her chest. Her breathing became ragged. Something about the way Ramona's eyes glared at her, even post-mortem, frightened her.

Standing ankle deep in the hole, Charlotte gasped. Her shovel fell as she dropped to her knees beside the woman.

"Oh my God." She took hold of the woman's hand, its chill making her nauseous. Looking around, she saw she was alone outside. Last she remembered, she had been running down the gravel driveway. Her eyes scanned the woman, from her blown apart scalp to the deep cavity in her chest. She smelled of pennies and shit, and with a start, she realized this was Ramona.

The front door opened, and she flinched.

"What did you do?" she screamed, tears flowing down her face.

He raised an eyebrow as he strutted over. "What do you mean, Bethany?"

Frustration built in the back of her throat. "I'm not Bethany!" She cried into her hands and shouted again. "I'm not Bethany!"

He rushed over to her, confused.

"I'm the missing girl! I know it!" She looked at him from between her dirty fingers. Pointing up to him, she screeched, "You stole me! I'm the missing girl from California! The police—"

He clamped a hand over her mouth, pressing her face into it with a hand on the back of her head. "And how are you going to prove that?"

Charlotte looked up to his burning eyes, tears dripping onto his clean hand. Her teeth painfully dug into her lips.

"Do you even remember anything?" he asked, a wide smile exposing his pale, pink gums.

She looked down at the woman in front of her and shook her head.

"Do you know who Charlotte is?"

She shook her head again.

"You're Bethany."

Charlotte knew the name was not her own. Taking a chance, she shook her head again.

He shoved her down, forcing her into the mud and filling her ear. He spoke through his teeth into the other. "You're Bethany, and if you don't start acting like her again, I'll beat you until you do." He reeled back, punching her in the ribs.

She gasped, looking into the old woman's dead eyes.

With Ramona buried, Neil told Charlotte to clean up. In the bathroom, she closed the shower curtain, refusing to step inside. The uncertainty of it made her nauseous. She soaked a hand towel and worked on wiping the mud from her face and out of her ear at the sink.

The mirror gave the image of Bethany, but she didn't *feel* like Bethany.

The brown bob cut made her look old, but she didn't feel old. The heavy makeup still on half her face made her look proper, but she didn't feel proper. It itched on her skin, even after wiping it off. The clothes she wore felt confining although baggy, as if she was wrapped in loose chains.

A pair of scissors glinted at her from a cup containing a comb, tweezers, and cotton swabs. She swirled her head side to side, watching the short hairs lift up like the skirt of a dancer.

Her eyes glanced to the doorknob of the bathroom. She was sure there was supposed to be a lock, but the knob was smooth, reflecting back at her a distorted image of herself, not that the image in the mirror was any clearer. Shrugging, she snatched up the scissors. She plucked a lock of hair free from above her forehead and wildly swung at it with the two open blades. In a snip, the hair was on its slow journey to the floor. A tuft oddly stuck up from the rest of her uniform haircut, begging her to cut the rest.

Pulling up a handful of hair, Charlotte carved at it with the scissors. Hair rained down to her feet. She smiled, shredding through another chunk, then another, and another. When all the long strands were cut, she ruffled it about, trimming the fluffy, standing strands evenly about her head. Using the brush covered in brown hair that was not her own, she brushed it back away from her forehead. Not liking this, she brushed it straight up, pulling the sides out with her fingers. She enjoyed the chaos of the look, resembling an angry brown ocean of tumultuous waves.

"Dinner!" Neil called, startling her into dropping the scissors.

She quickly scooped up what hairs she could, dumping them into the trash. Slinging off her clothes, she threw the wet towel this way and that across her body, scrubbing away the now-dried mud.

"I said dinner!"

She slipped on the nightgown he had hastily handed her, realizing it was lingerie. The bra was too small, squishing her breasts in a way she knew he would notice. She grimaced at how the lace flowed over her hips, exposing the underwear beneath. Her breath came and went quickly, making her head buzz as she hyperventilated.

He hammered his fist against the door. "It's going to get cold!"

She threw open the door, meeting his surprised eyes. He stepped back from her, in awe of the sight. Drinking in her body, he smirked. "Don't you look—"

Bethany's fist found his jaw, sending him flat on his back. "Don't you rush me!"

He looked up at her, the taste of pennies slick on his torn tongue. "What's your name?" he asked, cowering.

"Bethany, you *fuck*." She stomped past him and into the kitchen. Opening the fridge, she asked, "Where's my sweet tea?"

He stood and walked into the kitchen, cowering. "On the table, dear."

Most of the meal was spent in silence as he stared at Bethany, watching as she ate like a wild boar.

"What happened to your hair, dear?"

She snapped her eyes up to him. "My what?" Her hand reached up to grasp her chin length hair, and her fingers searched her bare neck until they reached behind her ear. Eyes wide, she ran her hands over her freshly chopped hair. "Oh, god."

Getting up knocked her chair over, and she almost tripped on it as she rushed to the master bathroom. Her reflection showed a woman she didn't recognize.

"Neil!"

Her face flushed red as she stormed down the hallway, meeting him at the end. Although smaller than him in width and stature, she lay her hands on his shoulders and shoved, knocking him down on his ass. "How could you do this to me?!"

He lay sprawled out in front of her, a faint smile on his lips.

She thrust her foot into his groin, hoping it would bust through it.

A wide grin broke out on his face as he curled into a ball. "Do it again," he groaned.

She scrunched her nose with a gasp, skirting around him. *Fresh air. Fresh air. Get me out of this fucking house.* She latched onto the doorknob, twisting it to no avail. "Neil, come unlock this door, now!"

He appeared from the hallway, fully undressed.

"What are you doing?" she asked, jiggling the doorknob.

"Bethany, you're a domme." He shook his head, placing his hands over his face, then pleaded at her. "Please remember. I've been so lonely since your accident."

She raised an eyebrow at him.

"Come with me, please."

The sadness in his voice enraged her. She followed at a distance.

Neil led her to the bedroom and showed her the straps which dangled from the bedposts. "You strap me here, and," he paused, smirking, "you get to do whatever you'd like with me."

Images flashed through Bethany's mind of the kind of torture she could put him through, but a thought provoked her. "And you like this?"

He hopped onto the bed. "It's *all* I think about." He lay flat, his wrists and ankles near the restraints. "Tie me up, Pussykat."

Bethany smiled, slipping the restraints onto him and cinching down.

"Now go to the closet and get the whip."

Slipping and into the bathroom rather than the closet, Bethany retrieved his straight razor from the bathroom counter, along with a bottle of aftershave. She held them behind her back, smiling. Standing over him, she asked, "You can't get out of those?"

He shook his head, his face relaxed in bliss.

Bethany reeled back, slamming her empty fist into his ribs. He coughed, trying to regain his breath, when she whipped the straight razor out from behind her back.

His eyes widened. "What—what are you going to do with that?" He pulled on his wrist restraints, wriggling and writhing as she inched closer to his exposed abdomen with the glinting blade. He screamed, desperately trying to pull away from her.

In a flash, a thin crescent of crimson appeared just under his belly button. He sucked air in through his teeth, finding the pain unsatisfactory.

"*Cherry!*" he yelled as she dragged the blade up from his belly button to the center of his chest, digging a fine line throughout. Beads of blood dribbled out, following the curve of his abdomen to his crotch. "*Cherry!*" he called again.

She laughed. "Honey, my name is," she slashed the blade across his chest, nearly missing his nipple, "*Bethany.*"

He yelped, the slash cutting deep.

In large swoops and curves, Bethany carved her name into his side, listening to his cacophony of screams. Each line gently bled as she barely broke the surface.

As she finished the long tail of the Y, she brought the blade up to his neck, slicing into the thin skin.

The aftershave whispered to her from the sheets next to his writhing thigh, so she set down the blade and unscrewed the cap, setting it over his nose. She flung the bottle around, dousing him in a shower of green rain.

He screamed as the liquid seeped into his wounds, burning him from the inside out.

Picking up the blade once again, Bethany held it to his throat, putting more and more pressure on it.

"*Why are you doing this to me?!*" he screamed, straining against the blade.

Her heart thudded in her chest, thundering in her ears. She smiled, penetrating the skin further. Bethany was sky high.

But Charlotte looked deep into his pain-filled eyes and screamed. Dropping the blade on his chest, her eyes took in her blood-soaked hands and his carved, naked body.

You are responsible.

She ran out of the room, bolting down the hall to that bright-red front door. Her bloodied hands slipped around the locked knob as she cried. Head spinning, she ran to the back door, dodging broken glass and shoving her shoulder against the plywood. She struck it over and over, pain flaring up on her side. Wiping away tears, she sat on the cold tile, bloody shards of glass surrounding her.

Neil cried from the bedroom, his sobs loud in her ears. "Bethany, help me."

Charlotte covered her ears, forcefully scrunching her eyes closed. She cried her own tears. *Who am I? What did I do?*

Sniveling, she uncovered her ears. Neil's crying took precedence in her mind as she stood up. She sighed. The back of her head throbbed while she cautiously wandered into the back of the house.

On tiptoes, she entered the bedroom, finding him sobbing in his restraints. She looked them over, and with a heavy beating heart, she slowly unclasped each one, releasing him.

He held his arms out to her, still crying, and, with uncertainty, she embraced him. He held her close as he lay down, her head pressed against his bleeding chest.

Through their tears, he whispered, "*I only wanted to love you.*"

Eight

Ew.

Charlotte woke in his arms, sticky with blood, sweat, and tears. She crawled out from under his grasp, creeping to the front of the house. Ducking into the guest bath, she grabbed a washcloth and scrubbed herself free of his blood and scent.

With the TV as low as she could listen, she tuned in to the local news channel. Weather, an interview with an author, and a segment about the local animal shelter came on, but nothing about a missing girl.

She sighed, resting her face in her hands. Her eyes landed on Neil's phone, and her heart skipped a beat. It was in her hand before she knew it, and she thanked him for not having a password.

It can't be this easy.

Tapping the search bar, she typed in, *Charlotte Brenagan*, unknowingly misspelling her own last name. Search results came up for *Charlotte Brenegan*, and she quickly tapped the name.

"Missing California Woman May Be Tied to Sex Trade."

"Young Californian Girl Taken in Plain Sight."

She scrolled past the articles, looking for an image.

Finally coming across one, she felt awestruck. Charlotte had long, blonde hair, big brown eyes, and a smile a mile wide. Her teeth were straight and white. A tear came to her eye when she realized this girl could be dead.

Or she could be me.

A chill trailed up her spine. She stood up, rushing to the guest bath. Holding the phone up next to her reflection, she smiled. Although it was a strained, painful smile, she realized how much she resembled the woman.

The tooth gap was exactly the same. A crinkle next to her right eye appeared just as the one on Charlotte's face.

I need to get help.

She almost hit herself for wasting time in the mirror instead of calling the police. There had been a fog over her mind for the minimal days that she could remember. Exiting the camera app, the doorknob jiggled.

"Good morning, Bethany," Neil cooed from the other side.

Her finger slipped, opening his recent tabs, all of which contained something about Charlotte Brenegan.

The door opened, revealing Neil's smiling face and naked, bloody body.

She gasped, dropping his phone in the sink.

"*What are you doing?*" His hand landed in her short, dark hair, barely gripping the strands, and yanked.

She screamed as his fingers curled in her hair, pulling her to the floor.

"*Nosey little bitch!*" he yelled as he dragged her out of the bathroom. Down the hall and through his bedroom, he opened up her side of the his-and-hers closet, exposing a wire dog kennel. He pulled her face close to his. "What's your name?"

Hot tears ran down her red face as she whispered, "Charlotte Brenegan."

His eyes widened, and he forced her into the cage. "I hate you!" He pulled at the lingerie. "Take it off!"

She landed on her stomach, scrambling to turn around and face him. His fingernails raked scratches into her skin as he pulled at the nightgown. Finally turned around, she kicked at him. The nightgown tore under his force, and he yanked it free of her body, leaving her in underwear that were too tight for her. She pushed herself to the corner of the cage as he reached in farther.

Without thought, she lunged out and bit him, digging deep into his arm. His fist found her eye, making her release him. As she caught her bearings, he clutched onto the underwear and pulled them free. Tossing them aside, he slammed the cage closed, locking the attached padlock.

He stared in at her, arm dribbling blood. "If you don't start acting like Bethany more often, I'm going to kill you."

She held her swimming head in one hand. "So, I'm not Bethany?"

"You are, but there's also an entire world of vulnerable women out there."

She thrust her fingers through the cage, the tips just poking into his eyes.

Grabbing his face, he yelled, "Fuck you!" and slammed the closet door shut, leaving her in darkness.

She felt the onset of tears but shoved them down. *No use in crying. Crying is for relief, and I'm far from that point.*

The blackness swallowed her whole, leaving her to feel hollow and void. Nothing but her own breathing tickled her ears, but her mind raced on. She was certain she was not Bethany. *What man would treat his wife so badly?*

Thinking through the past few days, she couldn't recall a solid memory. Everything was nothing or clouded over.

How did I end up with him on the bed?

She curled her knees to her chest, hugging them close.

And what was I doing with the knife?

Conflicted feelings rose between feeling vulnerable as she sat naked in a cage, or feeling safe, the darkness hiding all that she currently was.

She sat still for hours, seeming to hear and feel every movement within her body. The blood rushing through her veins was loud in her ears and hot in her limbs, pumping fiercely under her chilled skin. She felt her lungs expand and contract with every breath, noticing how she rasped with each exhale. Her stomach lolled around, sick and empty. The back of her head was wet and oddly warm.

Feeling brave, she reached into the dark, unable to even see her hand. Her fingers grazed the bars, and she wrapped her index finger around one. In an effort to stop the thoughts from racing around her mind like angry hornets, she counted each bar as she felt it. *One, two, three...*

The closet door swung open, bathing her in a blinding ray of light from the bathroom's fluorescent bulbs.

"Get out and get dressed, *now*," Neil said, unlocking the padlock.

She remained deep in the cage, comfortably away from his grasp.

On his hands and knees, he dragged her out by her ankle. "You had better be dressed in five minutes."

She looked up to him, unmoving.

"Say anything, and you *die*." He stormed out of the room, closing the bedroom door behind him.

Laurence Brenegan waited in the front entranceway.

"How is she, Neil?"

"Ah, she's doing better. She should be out soon. You know *women*," he said with a chuckle, moving a pretend lipstick around his mouth.

"So, there's been a lead to Charlotte."

"Really?"

"Yes, a house was found in California." Laurence paused, shaking his head. "So far they've found a whole basement system full of bodies."

Neil gasped.

"It was some sick game to this bastard." Laurence sighed, clearly distraught. "They think she was taken there but haven't discovered her body yet."

"That's both wonderful and terrible news to hear," Neil said, hand on his hip casually.

"Yeah, I just thought I would let you know, and—"

Charlotte stared at her reflection, all bruised and pale. Her eye had swollen quickly, but she could still see through it. Something glinted in the corner of her vision.

There sat the straight razor, still coated in blood.

She heard voices and quickly turned away from the mirror.

Bethany looked down at herself, unsure how she had gone from killing Neil to naked in the bathroom. The back of her head and eye throbbed. Voices piqued her interest. She dug through his side of the closet, searching for a clean flannel.

I thought I killed this motherfucker.

Dressed in a flash, she scurried to the bedroom door, cracking it and listening. *Laurence. That bastard.* Certain Neil called the police on her, she fled back to the closets, rummaging around Neil's side. *He has to have something here.*

Tossing aside his clothes, she spotted a light. Just a crack of light, so faint she almost mistook it for a trick of her eyes. Looking closer, she pressed a hand against the wall, pushing inward.

The small room felt oddly familiar in a way she couldn't explain. Entering the small space, she took in the sights. The women on the walls disgusted her, and she was sure Neil was behind the camera in every one of the photos. The blue light of the computer gave shape to something dark contrasted against the light carpet.

Bingo.

In the bedroom, she waited, overhearing bits and pieces of their words.

"—*you in Redding. That's where Charlotte was taken, Neil.*"

"*I know I was seen with a woman, but—*"

Her breath stopped, and she leaned farther out of the door, trying to hear the end of his sentence. Jealousy fueled anger flooded her. *Another woman? The hussy Ramona was talking about. Maybe the old bat was on to something.*

On light feet, she crept down the hall, her hands behind her back. She had dressed nicely in a blouse and skirt, playfully throwing on one of Neil's flannels over top. Slipping around the corner and into Laurence's view, she smiled.

He scanned over her appearance, finding the new haircut and skirt odd. "Hi, Bethany," he said with a tight-lipped smile. The black eye set off every alarm in his head.

In less than a breath, the pistol was out from behind her back. A millisecond passed as she aimed with her black eye scrunched shut and pulled the trigger.

Before Neil could tear his eyes away from him, a spray of blood erupted from Laurence's throat, sending him into the wall. He slid down, leaving a trail of crimson above his head. Wide-eyed, Laurence gripped his throat, gurgling and choking.

Neil spun around from his place on the couch, meeting the barrel of his own pistol. "What the fuck, Bethany?!"

"I thought I slit your throat, you son of a bitch."

Laurence gasped his final breaths as they spoke. "What's wrong with you?" he asked, frozen in front of the gun.

She moved toward the front door, where the dead cop lay, a river of blood pouring from his neck. "Get in the goddamn car." She grabbed the keys from their hook, still aiming at Neil.

He stared at her from the couch.

"*I said get in the goddamn car!*"

She drove slowly, rolling over the gravel road at a snail's pace. Neil trembled in the passenger seat, his eyes on the gun in Bethany's lap. She fiddled with the car's navigation system, swerving this way and that across the road.

"Where are we going?" he asked softly.

She typed in the city as he watched, his heart sinking into his stomach. "We're going to California," she responded, smiling.

Her expression hurt Neil's head, so he panned down to the gun again. "Why?"

"To see who this girl is."

"Who?"

"*Charlotte.*"

"Charlotte is just a missing girl from California, Bethany." He shook his head. "It has nothing to do with either of us."

"I heard you talking about her and about picking up another woman."

Neil sighed.

"Not as fucking invalid as you think I am, huh?" She tapped *Go* on the screen.

"*Turn left onto U.S. Highway 191.*"

The hours passed in silence. Bethany drove, appearing relaxed, as Neil contemplated jumping from the car. Images of him rolling on the rough asphalt, tearing open his flesh like a bloody, peeled banana flashed in his mind, keeping him within the tension of the car.

"I have to pee," he blurted.

She laughed. "Lucky for you, you can pee in a bottle." She retrieved a bottle from the back seat, not realizing it once contained the drugged water that helped bring her to Neil's home.

"I don't want to." He crossed his arms, looking in the side mirror—no cars in front or behind them. None were even passing by in this rural area.

Much like a girl he used to know, he struck out at her, causing her to steer into the next lane.

Grabbing the pistol, she put it to his temple without drawing her eyes from the road. "Keep it up, Neil. I don't need you on this mission."

He slapped at her arm, and without hesitation, she fired. He screamed as flesh ripped from his arm. The bullet entered the muscle, tearing away a good portion, and exited the car through the door.

Ears ringing, Bethany pulled over to the median of the highway, stopping the car amidst broken glass and blown apart tires.

Neil writhed in his seat, clutching his arm. Blood poured through his fingers in streams.

She reeled back, sending the butt of the gun onto the top of his head. She pulled back again, whipping his temple with the barrel. He grunted, falling against the door in a heap. A gentle drop of blood oozed from his freshly bruised temple as she rolled back onto the highway.

The headlights only illuminated so far, and Bethany's eyes were tired. Neil's presence kept her on edge the entire five hours he was asleep. Considering the darkness of the car keeping him hidden in the shadows beyond her peripheral vision, she decided to pull over and tie him up.

On the side of the road, she got out, basking in the coolness of the night. There were no lights besides the stars and her yellow headlights. Bending back into the car, she flicked on the interior light, illuminating a sickly looking Neil. Swooping to the other side, she opened the door, letting his head fall to the gravel. His body followed suit, slumping him beside the car. She had noticed a small string of rope just poking out under the passenger seat some hours ago and thought it would do.

She flipped him onto his belly and tied up his ankles first.

A quick search of the dimly lit trunk had her walking away with two bungee cords and another string of rope.

A lot of tying materials for a pharmacist.

Taking the rope, she bound his wrists together behind his back. She knelt at his side, focused.

Finishing the knot, Charlotte stabbed herself under her thumb nail with her index fingernail, gasping. Cloudy minded, she stood up, unsure where she was. *If Neil is passed out, who drove us here?* She realized with a shudder that someone else was with them, and she was alone in the dark.

He groaned from under her, rolling onto his side. She jumped, hiding behind the car. She watched as he stood up, hopped farther to the side of the road, and yelled. "Bethany! Come untie me!"

I did that? Or is there another woman here?

Light approached behind her, steadily coming up the road. He turned around and hopped to the front of the car, wiggling around in the headlights. The car passed quickly, sending a fierce wind their direction.

"Bethany, goddamn it!" He struggled with the knot at his wrists, finding it looser than expected.

Charlotte shook her head, damning whoever tied him up as the rope fell from his wrists.

He bent over, untying his ankles. Looking in the car, he scoffed, finding the keys dangling from the ignition. "Fine! I'll just leave your ass here!"

She looked around, seeing nothing but ominous darkness waiting to swallow her whole. The moon laughed at her, its tiny sliver of light high in the sky. "Wait!"

He paused, just about to slip into the driver's seat. He smiled, his eyes shining.

She realized her mistake, bolting for the darkness beside the road.

He followed behind.

Tall grass tickled her legs as she ran downhill, and in a splash, she was down at the bottom of a ditch. Up to her waist in foul water, she waded about, hands searching for the other side.

He fell in behind her, sending a wave of icy water up her back. She grimaced, her hands finally landing on dirt. The embankment was steep. She had no purchase as her toes dug in and slipped. Her fingers clawed at the mud, penetrating the wet soil.

He wrapped his arms around her, dragging her backward. Lips on her ear, he whispered, "We've been here a hundred times before. Stop fighting."

She gritted her teeth, grunting, "Never." She threw her head back, slamming into his nose. She pulled forward and rolled to the side, tossing him underwater. As he let go, her hands searched for his neck, locking on with an iron grip.

If she weighed more or was even slightly stronger, she may have kept her balance.

He pushed up against her, forcing her into the water. Gasping, he snatched her arm. He pulled her face close to his, noses touching, and yelled, "I'll kill you! I swear to God, I'll kill you!"

Anger bubbled up inside of her. Hot tears forced themselves free, mingling with the cold, muddy water on her face. "What are you waiting for? Fucking do it already!" she yelled back, pressing her forehead into his like a challenging buck.

Swiftly, he grabbed her by the side of the head, forcing her skull into his knee that came roaring out of the water.

Limp in his arms, she dreamed of a home she didn't know was hers.

Nine

Am I in a refrigerator?

Charlotte opened her eyes to a dank basement only lit by a flashlight on a staircase. Sheet-covered furniture and concrete walls surrounded her as she discovered she was chained to the legs of a dusty grand piano. The heavy chain was clumsily wrapped about her ankles and wrists, loose enough to move but not enough to remove.

As she struggled with the rusty chains, one of the large wooden doors opened. The night stared at her for a moment before Neil hopped down the stairs, a woman across his shoulders.

"Who is that?" she asked, her voice high.

"This is *Bethany.*"

She shook her head, thinking of the girls she had seen on the walls of his hidden room.

He laid the woman in a damaged clawfoot tub in the corner of the basement and dragged over a chair. A wide grin took up half his face as he pulled out a small pair of rusty scissors from his pocket and propped her up.

"Isn't her hair the prettiest shade of brown already?" he asked, stiffly turning to face Charlotte. His hand was deep in the woman's hair, clutching it like a child would hold their favorite toy in the midst of fear. "Unlike someone else's." He snipped the scissors in the air twice before pulling out a strand of the unconscious woman's hair. It spanned the length of his arm until he chopped it off at the base of her neck.

She watched as he repeated the process, covering the floor by his feet with the woman's hair.

Bile threatened to force itself up her esophagus as she imagined him cutting off her pretty blonde hair and dyeing it brown.

With a cautious tone, she asked, "Who is Bethany?"

"Well, she's my wife," he said, brushing the woman's fresh bob cut with his fingers. He bent over and dug around in a bag at his feet, which she had seen in the trunk, until he produced a bottle of foundation. She watched as he squirted a bit onto his finger and smeared it around on the woman's face. Even in the dim light of the flashlight she could see it didn't resemble the woman's skin tone a bit.

"Where is she?" she asked, keeping her tone flat.

"Bethany?" he asked in return, dabbing more foundation onto the woman's neck and shoulders.

"Yes."

His smile grew as he delicately applied red lipstick to the woman's lips. "Well, she's right in front of me." He slowly leaned in, his nose pressing into the woman's.

She averted her eyes as he applied the lipstick to himself, moaning. He circled his lips over and over, spreading it to his chin and nose. Smiling, he smeared it on his teeth, prodding it with his tongue.

"Bet you're jealous," he said.

She looked at him again, grimacing at how the lipstick had smudged around his lips like blood. She shook her head. "Yeah, real jealous." She laughed. "Cuz she's unconscious and I had to watch that." She laughed again, expecting him to come at her with a heavy hand.

Startling her, he burst into laughter himself, slapping his knee. "You're just lucky you're not my concern anymore."

"What do you mean by that?" Her heart fluttered at the thought of not being his concern.

"Well, I have my wife to think about. Can't be living with another woman. No, no."

She leaned her back against the piano leg, confused. "Am I Charlotte Brenegan?"

He stood up, tight-lipped. He retrieved a loaf of bread from his bag and slowly approached her. "No."

Tilting her head up to look at him, she asked, "Then who am I?"

His smile was gentle and genuine this time around. "Why, you're *Clover*." He took a piece of bread out and dangled it over her head. His lips twitched, sending his smile into that of a maniac briefly, then back. "You were injured in the same accident as Bethany. I'm just so glad the veterinarian helped get you healthy again." He dropped the bread in front of her, then ruffled her hair. She watched as his eyes lost focus, his hand still in her hair. Under his breath, he said, "Too bad you lost your ears in the accident."

What the fuck?

Charlotte, although disgusted with herself, picked up the bread as soon as he turned around. She scarfed it down, hoping to ease the constricting boa that was her stomach. Licking her fingers, she heard a gasp.

"*Where am I?*" The woman sat up in the bathtub, wide eyes looking around.

"You're in hell," Charlotte said, wiping her lips with the back of her hand.

Neil spun around, smacking her on top of the head.

"Don't mind the dog, honey." He slunk over to the woman, pressing his palms against her cheeks and gazing into her eyes. When she pulled away from him, he tightened his grip, digging his fingernails into her jawline. "My sweet PussyKat." He sighed, dropping his hands from her face.

"My name is Regina," she whispered.

Charlotte inhaled sharply, expecting him to strike the woman.

A second surprise came when he laughed. "We're going to call you PussyKat for now."

The door to the cellar opened. A man with ruffled gray hair stood dumbfounded at the sight of them all.

"Help!" Regina screamed, before Neil's hand clamped over her mouth.

"Who are you people?" the man asked, his voice light and curious, anything but alarmed.

Neil spoke first, struggling to keep PussyKat within his grasp. "I'm Neil. This is my wife, PussyKat, and our dog, Clover. She'll run away if the door's open. That's why we had to chain her." He smiled.

Charlotte waited for the man to completely lose himself, call the police, and end her suffering.

His pale face split into a grin wider than Neil's had ever been.

"I've always wanted a family," he said.

Silence.

Charlotte's heart beat heavy in her ears.

As the man pulled a shotgun from behind his back and aimed it at Neil, Charlotte realized something.

There exists people crazier than Neil, and death may be my only way out.

"Come with, Daddy. Bring Mommy with."

Neil stared at the man, wide-eyed.

"Let's go."

Not taking his eyes from the shotgun, Neil pulled PussyKat from the bathtub. Pushing her in front of him as they exited the basement, they were swallowed up by the darkness outside.

Charlotte took a deep breath. Looking at her chains, she knew she didn't have the strength to pick up a grand piano, and they were wrapped too tightly around her wrists and ankles to remove them.

The cellar door opened, creaking loudly. The strange man walked in, a dog leash and empty collar hanging over his shoulder. His shotgun dangled loosely from his grasp as he approached.

Charlotte backed herself into the piano leg.

The man bent over, his face close to hers. His breath stunk of rotten tuna fish, and she grimaced as he spoke. "I've always dreamt about having a doggy." He slipped the collar around her throat, cinching it loose enough so she could breathe. "Gee whiz, a puppy all for me."

He pulled a bobby pin from his own mane of thunderhead-like hair, quickly unlocking the padlock holding her chains. He gently unwrapped them from her limbs, patting her hair. "Don't worry, I'll take care of you," he cooed.

As he pulled her away from the piano, she didn't know whether to stand on two feet or stay on all fours. The shotgun in his hand whispered threats to her, so she remained on all fours.

Being entirely exhausted she slowly crawled behind him. Had she any energy left in her body, she would have fought him, or so she thought. Compared to Neil, she felt a strange sense of security with this calm, older man.

She didn't trust it.

Pink and orange light filtered through the trees around the old home as the sun peeked over the horizon. The house's two stories were covered in beaten boards as gray as the man's weathered hair. Each window had at least one crack or hole in it, and the door didn't look like it would hold back even a fly. The gravel-filled dirt hurt her knees and palms, but more than anything, she was glad to be out of Neil's cramped house.

The wet smell of moist dirt and damp outside air clung to her nose. She breathed it in deeply, sure she wouldn't have a chance soon.

He opened the front door, revealing a dark entryway full of dirty, old shoes, all ranging from pink newborn slip-ons to big, battered leather boots.

Others?

He kicked some aside to let her in, closing the door with a slam. "This way, girl." He gently pulled on her leash, guiding her down a long hallway.

Through the darkness, she could see the vintage, gray wallpaper drooping down in strips. They waved down at her as she passed. She wondered how many others these strips had watched or if she was part of the first group.

Looking around his legs, Charlotte spotted a bright light peeking behind a door at the end of the hallway. He sped up, pulling her along, and opened it. There Neil and PussyKat sat, tied up to wooden chairs. Each had a matching, filthy rag bound around their mouths.

"Mommy and Daddy are in timeout." He shook his head, looking down at Charlotte. "They tried to hurt me with words."

She blankly stared up at him, her attention fanning out as she longed for sleep.

"Sticks and stones may break my bones, but words can never hurt me," he mumbled. Abruptly, he heartily laughed, sounding like a child as he clutched his belly, then he was very still. His deep, dark eyes looked down at her again, burning two matching holes into his pale, crepey skin. "You won't try to hurt me with words, will you, Doggy?"

She stared up at him, her bladder almost giving way.

A smile cracked his face in two. "Of course not! Doggies don't talk."

He pulled her over to a couch, sitting down and patting the seat that was as gray as his hair, as gray as the rest of the home. Charlotte cautiously climbed onto the dingy cushion, the must almost unbearable.

"You said she'll run away if we don't tie her up, right?"

Neil nodded, biting down on his gag. Tears wet his cheeks, soaking the rag.

The man took the leash, bent over, and gently tied it to the leg of the couch.

Not that I can't remove this collar, but okay.

Charlotte tried to lay like a dog, keeping her elbows under herself and feet tucked in tight. The cushion tingled under her exposed flesh, making her skin crawl. She could see the front door from where she sat but couldn't imagine what this man would do to her if she tried to run.

"Well, since you're my parents," he paused, looking at Charlotte and winking, "you should already know this, but my name is Peter." He fiddled with his hands in the silence and blurted, "And you'll be staying here for the rest of your lives."

Regina's eyes widened. She shifted in her chair, trying to speak through the rag.

He smiled and relaxed into the couch, staring at the couple. His wild hair and sharp stubble shone from the fluorescent light above them, the light being the only thing in the home that appeared new.

Charlotte kept her head straight, her eyes glued down the long hall toward the door. Her arms began to burn, trembling as she held herself up.

"Aw, Doggy is cold." Peter giggled, grabbing a blanket from the floor.

Charlotte watched the dirt roll off the yellow-and-brown stained blanket as he picked it up and draped it over her. What once was a soft material was crunchy and hardened by things only Peter knew. Charlotte shivered again, this time as she held burning bile from escaping her throat.

Peter stood up, slowly walking toward Neil. He took his steps slowly, methodically. He loomed behind Neil with a grin, his hands slowly reaching for the man's neck. Neil gasped as the rag was untied, falling onto his lap. Peter did the same to Regina, returning to his place on the couch, only closer to Charlotte. He idly put a hand on her back, stroking it as he spoke. "What's your name?" he asked, looking at Regina.

"Neil."

Peter snapped his eyes to him. "Yes, *Daddy*, I know your adult name, but I was asking Mommy."

Regina appeared to have seen a ghost, her lips clamped shut as she chewed her cheek.

"*Mommy*, what's your name?" Peter's gravelly voice cracked as he tried to pitch it higher.

"R—Regina," she said, looking over at Neil.

"Reegeenaw," Peter said, a goofy smile on his face. A droplet of drool clutched his gray lip.

Charlotte looked over his sharp features and how his skin sagged on every angle.

"What's Doggy's name?" he asked, petting Charlotte's head.

"Clover," Neil said matter-of-factly.

Peter snapped his head down to look at Charlotte, a frown on his lips. Speaking slowly, he said, "What's Doggy's name?"

Charlotte stared deep into the man's eyes, his pupils indiscernible from his dark irises. "Charlotte," she whispered.

"Charlotte?" His frown spread into another grin, and he nodded. "I like Charlotte." He gave her a big, clumsy hug, suffocating her with the scent of rotted meat.

Charlotte watched from the kitchen floor as Peter cut up rotted vegetables and dumped them into a large pot. Her leash was tethered to the small breakfast table that was littered in stacked newspapers, and she strained to see every ingredient Peter plopped into the pot. From Charlotte's view on the ground, she thought she saw the tail of a rat dangling from his cutting board.

"Mommy and Daddy gave me this job. It's very important that I do good."

Legs tired, Charlotte sat on her knees, crumbs and dirt painfully pressing into the thin skin. She centered more weight onto her hands, her fingers dangerously close to a sloppy brown stain. A noise came from the right, piquing her attention.

In the dining room sat a long, clothed table, the once-white linen turned to a sickly yellow. Neil and Regina sat at their places, tied to two tall chairs. Their feet swung down from the high perches enough so that Charlotte could pass under on all fours without touching. Regina was gently crying.

Charlotte turned her gaze back to Peter, looking up at him as he sliced into a squishy zucchini.

"Hmm." He scooped up a bit with his index finger and licked it off, sucking on it for a second before popping it out. Like a trained chef, he located a glass baking pan and stuffed in three rotten zucchinis, each topped with a few patches of white fuzz. With a fork, he mashed them down, then hastily tossed them into the oven.

"Bathroom?" Charlotte asked, just under her breath.

Peter stopped chopping on a lump of still bleeding flesh and turned to face her. "Doggy goes on the newspaper." Using the dripping knife, he pointed to a thick mat of stained, crinkled newspapers.

Charlotte crawled over, piss about to run down her thighs. She yanked down her underwear, leaned back on her toes, and let go. She was thankful for the privacy her skirt provided but didn't remember putting it on.

A cracked mirror faced her, showing her shameful image. *Who am I?*

"Doggyyyy," Peter said, watching over Charlotte, "that's a lot of pee pee, Doggy." He laughed, poorly imitating an infant's laugh. Charlotte cringed.

He returned to carving the bloody piece of meat on the counter as Charlotte wiped herself off with the cleanest available piece of newspaper, all the while keeping her skirt from falling in the fresh puddle.

From the dining room floated in little whimpers. Charlotte crawled to the end of her leash, looking out at Regina. *The pain must've finally hit her.*

The woman cried harder, exposed and unable to cover her face with her hands.

Peter had taken hold of the meat just above Regina's right hip and flayed it off in a solid swoop. He thanked her for the nutrition. "I'm so grateful for Mommy," he muttered, tossing her meat into a cast-iron skillet. He threw on a cube of moldy butter, stirring it in methodically.

Charlotte's mouth watered as she watched Regina bleed.

"Here, Doggy." Peter dangled a strip of meat out to her.

She turned around and stared at it. The dripping meat trembled in his hand as he wiggled it toward her face.

"Get it, girl."

She shook her head, grimacing.

Peter pulled his arm back. "No meat?" He paused, and furrowing his brow, he thrust the flesh toward her face again. "*All doggies eat meat.*"

It slapped the tip of her nose, splattering buttery juices on her lip. She quivered, her stomach clenching in on itself like an angry fist. Opening her mouth, she allowed him to place the strip on her tongue. Even through the repulsion, she enjoyed the bite. Soft and chewy, but warm and savory. She swallowed gratefully, craving more.

Neil watched from the dining room table. "You're sick!"

Peter snapped his eyes up to him. "Daddy, don't yell at me. I won't give the doggy scraps anymore." He pouted, turning back to the stove. His hand reached up to a cabinet above his head, opening it and sourcing out a box without even a glance. He opened the flap and dumped in rat poison, humming as he stirred it in. Looking down at Charlotte, he said, "Sorry, doggy doesn't get any soup."

She sat on the tile next to him, staring up at his worn face as he concentrated on dinner. *Who are you?*

Charlotte lay on a pile of dirty jackets as Peter served his *parents*. He had let her off the leash, giving her a stern warning to stay in the room with him at all times.

Neil and Regina sat stiffly in their seats, their hands untied. Each refused to use them to eat. Peter stared at them over his plate of steak. Steaming bowls of rotted soup gave the couple nausea, and Regina held her side, her tears drying on her cheeks.

A half-eaten bowl of dog kibble sat next to Charlotte's bed. She looked at the jackets she lay on with a full belly. Each had its own personality, ranging from infant to adult and from high to low quality. She no longer questioned where the owners went.

"I worked really hard on dinner," Peter said quietly. His voice trembled. "Least you could do is try it." He heavily set his chin on his hand, lower lip sticking out.

Charlotte eagerly watched as Neil picked up his spoon. He set it down. "I'm really not comfortable—"

The shotgun dropped onto the table, having been hidden at Peter's leg.

Neil stared at him, slowly picking up his spoon and dipping it into the soup. It crept to his mouth, slipping between his lips as he grimaced.

Charlotte smiled.

Neil gagged, spitting out the soup.

Peter stood up, snatching the shotgun and aiming it at Neil. "*Swallow it!*"

Bethany watched as Neil ate soup in a place she didn't recognize. She looked around, feeling at the collar around her neck. "Fuck!"

Peter swiveled his aim to Bethany as she stood up.

"Wha—what the fuck is going on?" she asked.

Neil's eyes widened. "Bethany?"

Peter scoffed. "Who's Bethany?"

"I'm Bethany."

"But you're—"

"She's my wife!" Neil snapped. He breathed heavily, almost shaking.

"Regina is your wife," Peter said.

"Who?" Bethany's eyes fell on Regina. She approached the woman, under Peter's aim.

"Regina is my mommy, and Neil is my daddy."

Bethany laughed, running her fingers through Regina's short hair. "Honey, you're lost. Neil doesn't have kids." She looked over at Neil, her eyes boring into his. "Cuz I won't fuck him." She slipped her hand around Regina's chin, placing the other on the back of her head, and before the woman could protest, Bethany yanked.

The crunch thundered through the silence of the room. Regina's face fell into her bowl of soup, spilling it across the table.

"Charlotte, I can't believe you would do that," Peter said.

"I'm …" She hesitated, her head fuzzy.

"She's Bethany, damn it!" Neil yelled, straining against the sheet that held his thighs to the chair.

"Who are you?" Peter asked, his voice soft in comparison to his hard demeanor and the gun pointed at her.

She looked back and forth between the two, suddenly very sad. "I don't know." In this moment of confused melancholy, she asked, "Who are you? Who's Charlotte?"

"I'm Peter. And Charlotte, well, Charlotte is you," Peter said blankly.

She thought about all the lapses in her memory, sighing. Her fingers lightly trailed the goosebumps on her arms.

Peter smiled. "It's like two doggies in one!"

Bethany ripped the collar from her neck, throwing it in Peter's face. "I'm not your fucking dog."

He flinched and thrust the shotgun toward her, to which she didn't budge. "What're you gonna do, pussy boy?" she asked, stepping toward him. The barrel pressed into her collar bone.

"Well, I'll—I'll shoot you!"

Bethany snatched the gun away, almost surprised at the ease. She smirked, aiming it at Peter and pulling the trigger.

Click.

"You think there's bullets in there?" he asked, eyebrows raised.

"No," Bethany sighed, opening up the barrel. "I thought there were going to be *shells!*" She snapped the shotgun shut, grabbed it by the end of the barrel, and swung it like a baseball bat at Peter's head. Upon impact, he toppled over like a bowling pin, snoring as his head hit the ground.

She faced Neil, finding his seat empty. A quick scan of the room had her thinking she knew exactly where he was. Lifting up the tablecloth, she smiled. "Peek-a-boo!"

He screamed, backing away from her on all fours. She picked up an extra chair, hurling it at him just as he stood up. It struck him square in the chest, knocking him down, but before she could make it to the other side of the table, he scrambled to his feet, running for the door.

The afternoon sun hid behind clouds, further obscuring the small amount of light filtering in through the trees.

She followed him out on his heels as he ran for the tree line through garbage and old cars. Anger fueled her aching muscles as she charged on.

He could run faster than she thought, quickly disappearing into the thick brush. She followed, soon lost in the trees. Bethany stopped, taking a moment to breathe; the world spun around her.

Quick footfalls came from behind her, through the leaves. She swiveled just in time for Neil to tackle her. He took her to the ground and pummeled at her head. "*Your name is Charlotte Brenegan! Your name is Charlotte Brenegan! You're from California. Go away!*" he yelled as he beat the sides of his fists into her head.

Bethany covered her head with her arms as best as she could manage while under the weight of him. A feeling of hopelessness overcame her as her head swam. Looking up to him between blows, she saw the pure hatred he had for her in his bared teeth and fiery eyes.

For the first time, Charlotte whispered to Bethany. *It's the only way out.*

Bethany called back, *No. He can't do this to me.* Tears ran down her face as blood trickled into her eyes.

He reeled back, closing one fist over the other, high over his head.

Bethany took this moment to claw at him. Her fingernail caught his eyelid, ripping a small chunk free.

He grunted, holding his bleeding eye.

Confidence soared through her as she threw her weight onto him and twisted, straddling his abdomen. Her hands stretched around his throat, cinching tight.

He pulled at her hands, digging his fingernails into them and his throat.

"This time, *I won't let go.*"

She smiled, pulling her lips back tight against her gums, and leaned all her weight forward onto his neck. His eyes bulged, the white contrasting against the deep red of his skin. Purple saturated his lips as she forced her hands closed tighter. He writhed beneath her, trying to tip her to the side, but like a bull rider, she held on, digging her toes into the dirt.

Leaves flew as his legs kicked about. Bethany clenched her thighs tighter, leaning forward onto her hands. Neil grunted, his stomach convulsing as he struggled for air. He pawed at her. His strength was fading, evident in the way he gently pulled at her hair. In one last try, he slapped Bethany across the cheek, barely tapping her before his hand fell useless at his side. She braced herself further, feeling her thumbs sink deeper into his throat.

Her heart raced heavy in her ears as he took his final breath. There she waited, choking his dead body to assure herself he was, in fact, dead.

Letting go, her hands glowed red and ached. She fell over beside him, exhausted, and on the forest floor, she slept.

Ten

Ouch.

Charlotte's eyes popped open as something poked her ribs. Peter stood over her, a stick in hand. He was eerily calm. "We have to bring his body inside."

She backed away from him and sat up. "*Body?*"

Glancing to her left resolved her confusion. Neil lie there, his face purple and his bugged eyes staring glassily into the sky. She gasped, holding a hand over her mouth. The body stunk like nickels and shit.

"Killed him good," Peter said, smiling. He bent down gripping Neil by his ankles. "Only problem with strangulation is the meat can get tough, but we can make a stew with him."

"A stew?" she asked, both disgusted and oddly curious.

"Yes, I've got potatoes and carrots in the garden. Maybe a bulb of garlic and one onion somewhere, too."

In the daylight, Charlotte could see just how old Peter was. Even in his voice he sounded worn and tired. She looked around for a means of escape, finding never-ending trees in each direction.

"If you leave on foot, you'll die," Peter said matter-of-factly. Like he'd read her mind, he doubled down with, "No one escapes my house."

Her stomach curled up into her throat, a nauseous mix of fear and hunger.

"Come inside. We'll talk. Have wine. Dinner." He dragged Neil in the direction of the house. "Come now, before you change your mind." He winked, further confusing Charlotte. He no longer spoke like a child.

She remembered bits of Neil's death; flashes between her own rage and his struggle for control. She couldn't recall what it felt like, but she remembered watching, like she was a patron in a movie theatre, only the movie was her murdering someone.

Watching Peter drag him away, she was almost thankful for whatever was wrong with her head—for whatever had given her the strength to end Neil before he ended her. Nonetheless, guilt ate away at her insides.

They sat at Peter's dining room table, each with a cup of instant coffee. Neil's naked body hung from a meat hook in the kitchen. She watched as the last of his blood trickled into the trough.

"Why are you here, Peter?" She spoke softly. Despite Peter's thin, wiry frame, he'd picked Neil up, hung him, and slit his throat with ease. He sat across from her, eyes wide. She thought of him like a predator ready to pounce, so she kept her voice low.

"I grew up in this house. In fact, this house is all I know." He tight-lipped smiled at her. "I was twelve when my parents left. I had to learn to be on my own from then on."

Charlotte nodded.

"A man's car *broke down*," he used air quotes to accentuate his words. "So he made his way here. He was very weak by the time he showed up with a gas can. I shot him in the neck from around the corner of the house as he walked up the drive." He shook his head. "I hadn't had meat in two years at that point. Squirrels don't count."

Charlotte's fingers and toes felt numb as she listened to his story.

"I ate meat for months off that man. He saved me from perishing that winter." Peter abruptly stood up, causing her to jump. "Follow me."

He guided her down the hallway and to the stairs. They spiraled downwards into the dark. She couldn't imagine where he was taking her.

"My father was a hunter, but I use this a bit *differently*." He opened up the freezer door.

Bodies hung there. Humans. They dangled from the ceiling, their backs pierced by meat hooks. Others were stacked up head-high along the walls like sandbags waiting for a storm. A pile of infants sat in the corner closest to the door, all pale and blue. One faced her, its dark eyes seeming to judge her. They were all missing people, just like her.

What disgusted her most wasn't there in the basement, rather, it was in her head. A little voice, that sounded like yearning, asked,

"What do you think each one tastes like?"

Peter closed the door, a smile on his face. He saw exactly what he wanted to in her eyes.

"Dinner?" he asked.

Charlotte nodded.

"Cutting here to here," Peter pointed the knife from Neil's hip to his kneecap, "makes the best cut in my opinion." He smiled that sick, sad smile of his that would let anyone instantly know he's bonkers. "But I'm no chef." He moved the blade swiftly and with one precise swipe, he held a chunk of Neil's leg. Charlotte's eyes focused not on the dangling strip of tantalizing meat, but rather, on the section of bone peeking out.

I killed him.

Her heart hammered in her chest—maybe the caffeine or maybe the fear rising in her throat.

Coward, Bethany thought.

Peter stopped talking, noticing the hardened look in her eyes. "Bethany," he said.

"Call me Beth." She smiled, admiring the bruise on the side of Peter's head. "Sorry about that."

Peter was surprised. "Are you?"

She laughed. "No, but that's what normal people say."

Peter smiled, taking his cut of meat to a cutting board on the counter.

With Neil dangling from a meat hook only feet from her, Beth felt less angry. She stared at him, like he was a life-size art piece. "What's for dinner?" she asked.

"Neil stew."

Bethany's eyes widened. "You're going to eat him?"

In unison Peter, outside her head, and Charlotte, inside her head, said, "*We're going to eat him.*"

Neil's meat was chopped into chunks and tossed into a large pot, along with zucchini, carrots, garlic, onion, and potatoes. These looked fresher than the last meal he'd prepared. He dumped a heaping spoonful of powder in.

"Human bouillon," he said with a grin. "Proud of myself for figuring that one out."

"That's disgusting."

"It's *bitchin'*."

Beth laughed and a flash of hurt warped Peter's face.

"What? People don't say that anymore?"

"Not the cool ones."

He shook his head. "I used to be cool."

"I'm sure."

Peter narrowed his eyes at her from over his shoulder as he stirred the pot.

She laughed again. "I like your moxie, kid."

Peter grunted and returned his attention to the stew.

Rain beat at the windows. The house smelled of ash, dust, and human stew, but it was warm and the air was still. If one could forget Neil hanging upside down with his throat slit and the dead woman at the dinner table, it could almost feel like home.

"Hey, Charlotte," Peter said.

"I'm Beth."

"Hey, Charlotte."

"I'm *Beth*."

Peter whipped around, bloody knife in hand. "Well, bring out Charlotte!"

Beth remained in her seat. Peter's scrawny build didn't stir any feelings of fear. "It doesn't work that way."

Peter pouted, turning back to the stew. "Charlotte is nice,"

"Charlotte is a coward who was kidnapped by a weak man, and she fears *people*."

"*Don't* call her that." Peter's hands gripped the edges of the counter. "Neil was evil."

"Is that why you're going to eat him?" Beth smirked.

"No, we're eating him because he tastes good."

Beth's stomach turned.

"Oh, don't act like you don't have human in you right now." Peter sharply laughed.

"Liar." Beth's eyes narrowed. Her heart hammered in her chest.

"No lie. Charlotte ate part of the other Bethany."

Beth gagged, glancing over at Regina who still sat slumped with her head on a plate in the dining room.

"You killed her, but first Charlotte ate her." He shrugged.

Charlotte leaned back in her seat. Her heart was beating fast, but it slowed as she took a deep breath. "The stew smells great, Peter."

Peter smiled, facing away from her. He noted this exchange.

"Can I bleed her?" Charlotte asked, looking at the empty hook next to Neil. Peter nodded. She untied the woman, then grabbed rope and tied Regina's feet together, as she'd seen Peter do. She picked the woman up under her arms and dropped her on the floor. Charlotte dragged her easily, pulled the hook down to the rope, and hoisted Regina up like a giant tuna with a pulley by the fridge. She grabbed a knife from the counter, feeling its weight in her hands, and slit Regina's throat. A trickle of blood dripped down her neck, over her chin, and across her face, much to Charlotte's disappointment.

"Livor mortis. Her blood is no longer *fresh*," Peter said without looking away from the pot. "Don't worry. We'll cut her up soon. Soup's done."

They cleaned the dining room table and reset a few of the placemats. Peter stoked a fire in another room, which heated the entire house. He came back with soot on his nose. Charlotte sipped on more coffee as they waited for the soup to cool down. Steamy little tendrils floated up, sending earthy smells into the air. She was ravenous but waited patiently.

"Why have you stayed here alone so long?"

Peter, sipping on wine, mulled it over, glancing around the room to avoid Charlotte's eyes.

The wallpaper in the dining room was white; the tablecloth was white; chairs: white. The light coming in from the windows was gray. Dust had settled about thickly, caked up on parts of the table an inch deep. One could easily see the place where Peter sat nightly and the routine which he had in patterns in the dust.

Charlotte followed his gaze, landing on a black and white family portrait. The big hair and puffy jackets gave her the impression the photo was taken in the eighties. The cowboy hats and fake rifles might've offered an explanation as to why the photo had no color.

"They were supposed to come back."

A knife stabbed her in the chest, fresh tears rising to the surface of her eyes. She thought of her family, which only existed as silhouettes. She knew there were three of them, but nothing more.

Peter took a bite of his soup, tears dripping into it. He chewed Neil's meat carefully, considering its flavor and texture. His tense shoulders relaxed as he ate another chunk.

Charlotte didn't much feel like eating anymore, rather, she craved a sense of comfort and familiarity that a family might offer, but when she took a spoonful of broth and drank it, her appetite blossomed. She quickly ate a piece of Neil. The meat was brownish-gray and unappealing to look at, but on her

81

tongue, it was rich and fatty and most importantly: it was human. Her entire body tingled as she chewed. She imagined Neil yelling at her. All that tension and anger was now grinding between her teeth. She ate until the bowl was empty, and when Peter asked if she wanted seconds, she said yes, tears soaking her face. Peter gave her a bowl with extra Neil and watched the girl eat it with fervor. He figured that the man hadn't been feeding her while keeping her captive and internally chuckled because there was no doubt that Neil was feeding her now. He stood, taking Charlotte's empty bowl.

"Thirds?" he asked, petting her short brown hair.

She smiled, held her stomach, and said, "No, I'm stuffed."

Peter laughed and took the dishes into the kitchen. He brought out a plate of shortbread cookies. "Made these with the fat of a hiker and her boyfriend."

Charlotte's hand hesitated above the plate. Was it right of her to consume a human she didn't know? she wondered.

Peter nudged the plate at her. "Ethics aren't a question when it comes to survival."

Images of her fighting Neil came to mind, and she snatched a cookie and put it to her lips. It was flaky and buttery and sweeter than any cookie she'd ever had.

With full stomachs, the two gathered in the living room on a sofa in front of the house's main hearth. Under blankets, Charlotte leaned on Peter and they watched the flames flicker and dance. He put an arm around her: the first human he'd swore never to taste.

"I was twenty-four before I decided my parents were never coming home."

"How old are you now?"

"Forty-eight."

A long silence ensued, until Charlotte had a disheartening thought.

"Do you think *my* family is waiting for me?"

Peter nodded, squeezing her a bit tighter.

Her nose burned as tears wetted her eyes again. "I think I have to go home."

Peter turned to her and hugged her with both arms. "You do whatever feels right," he whispered.

Eleven

This place stinks.

Charlotte woke to Peter standing over her, a mug of coffee in either hand.

"Good morning, sunshine," he said, smiling in a way that made Charlotte's stomach clench.

The bed was itchy. Her pillow was itchy. The blanket was itchy. Everything itched.

"Do you have a shower?" she asked.

Peter nodded. "Yes, yes, you need one."

She laughed and stood up, still wearing the skirt and tight shirt Bethany had put on.

"I'll get you some better clothes, too."

They drank coffee in the kitchen.

"Where did they go?" Charlotte asked, gesturing to the empty meat hooks.

"Downstairs. The meat will spoil up here."

She nodded, thinking that Peter's way of life was odd.

You don't even remember your own way of life.

She agreed with that sentiment, the three silhouettes still in the back of her mind. All night she'd tried to think of what she liked. She decided she liked root beer, pizza, and when she saw the paintings in the room Peter let her sleep in, it stirred something in her. She liked the fine brushstrokes and the way the colors blended. In her hands, she had a feeling of muscle memory. Over the canvas, she ghost painted, recreating the brushstrokes she saw.

Peter sat across from her calmly, watching as she zoned out. She looked at him, making eye contact, and asked, "Why do you act like a child sometimes?"

He immediately averted his eyes to the table and fiddled with a fork. His shoulders came up to his neck as he spun the fork around and around.

"Sometimes I just like to pretend."

Charlotte felt bad for asking.

"Sometimes I see people who remind me of my parents and I like to pretend that they came back and that I'm still little and that someone cares about the things I do and achieve." Tears were streaming down his face. He took a deep breath, and, almost shouting, said, "*I just wish they'd come back.*"

He covered his eyes with his hands and got up. "Shower's upstairs," he said, running out of the room.

Charlotte could hear him run up the stairs and slam his bedroom door.

She sighed and finished her coffee.

The shower was the cleanest space she'd seen in the house. There was an assortment of soaps along the shelves and the counter. The tiles were clean. Even the curtains didn't stink when she stuck her head in to turn on the water. She didn't get an eerie feeling like the one in Neil's home gave her.

Although the bathroom door didn't lock, Charlotte undressed and got in. The water was hot, and as it sprayed her body, she felt like she was washing away Neil and all the memories of him. It was too bad he was all she remembered. She had hope that she could replace his memories with memories of her family.

Redding, California, she thought, trying to picture the town.

Upon getting out, she saw fresh clothes on the counter. Peter must've snuck in. She didn't feel like it was an invasion of her privacy, especially as she slipped on the comfortable jeans and t-shirt. The soft sweatshirt was the best part. She felt warm and comfortable and at peace.

Out in the hallway, she saw Peter. "I have to leave," she said.

Peter shook his head. "No, please." He ran down the hall from his door and hugged her. "Please don't leave me."

Her heart hurt. She didn't want to leave him. He had somehow become her everything, and as she hugged him, she made him a promise. "I'll come back for you, but right now, I need to find *my* family."

He let her go, looking into her eyes. "I understand." She could see that he understood but was still angry and hurt. "I have a car outback that you can drive."

"Thank you."

"Hungry?" he asked.

"Yeah." She stared out a grimy window in one of the bedrooms. The forest loomed out in the bleak day, calling to her, telling her to run home. "Where are we?"

"The outskirts of Utah," Peter said, leading her downstairs. "I don't know what town it is, but lots of tourists come through." He chuckled. "Lots of tourists and hikers."

Charlotte sat at the kitchen table and watched as Peter set up a portable grill. He hooked it up to a small propane tank. "Like I said, *lots of hikers*."

She nodded, thinking of all the travel-sized soaps in the shower and all the supplies Peter miraculously had.

"One time a grocery truck pulled into the driveway. Driver was lost." He nodded, smirking as he threw a few breakfast sausages onto the grill. "Yeah, I hadn't had chocolate cake in years, but that truck was just about full of everything I needed to start a bakery. I ate his body for months in cookies and pies and cakes. He was…a bit fat. Easy to render." He turned the sausages over as the flame licked between the bars.

Charlotte's mouth watered.

They ate eggs and human sausages and oatmeal in silence. She could see the tears threatening Peter's eyelids. They both wanted to savor their last meal together.

It ended much sooner than both of them wanted, and as Peter cleared the table, he said, "You're a good dog." He clumsily reached out and patted her hand.

She nodded, smirking. "I'm a good dog."

"Want this one?" Peter asked, pointing to Neil's car.

"No." Charlotte shivered. "No, I'll take that white car."

They stood in Peter's junkyard. Cars and trucks and semis were parked this way and that. Even a few bicycles and motorcycles stood motionless, frozen in time at the last place their owner ever existed.

Peter weaved through the cars, opening the white one's door and tossing her the keys.

"She's all yours." He smiled, his eyes dark.

"Thanks, Peter." She walked over to him, placing a hand on his shoulder. "I appreciate it."

His smile fell into a deep, over-exaggerated frown, and he ran into the house, sobbing.

She sat in the driver's seat, the interior cleaner than she expected. A purse, wallet, and shopping bag sat piled up in the passenger seat. She wondered what bodies those belonged to.

Putting the key in, she was surprised how quickly it started. The tank was full, and she decided Peter must take care of these cars when he wasn't eating people.

Not much else to do in a place like this.

She backed out of his junkyard, swerving around a doghouse, a rotted play structure, and a pickup truck on cinder blocks. The gravel road reminded her of Neil's driveway, and she hoped one day she would forget that life as much as she had forgotten her real life.

It was slow going, but she felt small amounts of weight release from her chest the harder she pushed the gas. She got up to forty, the car dipping and hopping as she hit potholes. At fifty, she drove through a small body of water in the road, fanning up a spray of mud. At sixty, she hit a curve, and coming around the bend, a little girl crossed the road. Charlotte swerved around her, slamming on her brakes when more children entered the road in front of her.

Skidding to a stop in the wet gravel, she noticed a school building up ahead. Her heart thudded heavily as she drove slow, their small, beady eyes on her. All saliva dried from her mouth as she breathed like an asthmatic on the edge of an attack.

Images of the dead children in Peter's freezer flashed through her mind, and suddenly all the children around her car were hanging from hooks, their skin gray and hair matted and stringy.

She clamped her eyes shut, rolling forward at a snail's pace when someone yelled.

A woman stood before her, clutching the hand of a small child in a raincoat. She bared her teeth, yelling at Charlotte before kicking the car's grill.

Bethany stomped the gas.

Charlotte braked, making the car hop toward the woman.

The woman's eyes flared open further as she went around the hood to the driver's window.

Charlotte gave the woman no time as she punched the gas. She looked in her rearview, watching the red-faced woman flail her arms and scream. The little girl at her side wailed cartoonishly.

Past the school, she sped up again. Signs for the Danger Cave State Park flew by her. Charlotte made a mental note of the signs, making sure she would never return, despite her promise to Peter.

She joined the freeway, crossing the border between Utah and Nevada. The sun beat in front of her, rising with every mile she drove. She thought it symbolic to drive into the sun.

It was dead quiet in the car. She sniffled, trying to push back tears. The road blurred as she cried, and she smeared the tears away with the sleeve of the soft sweatshirt Peter had given her. The only thing she knew herself as was a killer—a killer that ate human meat. She couldn't remember her family. Those three silhouettes hadn't gotten any clearer. She couldn't even remember how old she was or what she did for fun. But she could remember that eating other humans was wrong.

It filled her with anxious guilt—the kind that makes stomachs clench and fingers shake. Her head hurt, yet all she could think about was getting her next fix. Charlotte couldn't imagine killing a human herself.

By the time she exited the freeway an hour later, her sleeves were soaked. She pulled into a gas station and up to a gas pump before fiddling around with the wallet. A fat wad of cash poked out of the pocket. She smiled. Looking in her visor mirror, Charlotte saw the mess she was. She straightened her short hair, pushing it down and removing the occasional piece of dandruff. Baring her teeth, she noticed a chunk of meat stuck by her canine. She sucked on it, trying to pull it out as she opened her door and stood up.

Every face in the gas station appeared to be on her. The woman at the pump ahead of her turned around, glaring. Charlotte read her shirt. *Murderer* was written in bright-red cursive. She looked away, spotting a couple side-eyeing her, and glanced back at the woman, noticing her shirt actually read *Midlifer*. The woman smiled, quickly looking away.

She locked the car door with the key, quickly walking to the front of the convenience store. People were watching. She clutched the wallet tightly to her hip, her eyes swiveling from side to side.

Waiting in line, she frequently shifted her weight from one foot to the other, fidgeting with her short hair in the meantime. She pulled out the strands, pushed them down, then pulled them out again, running her fingers up and down the back of her head.

It didn't occur to her that she remembered simple things like driving, filling up the car, or waiting in line. All that was on her mind was *not* being recognized.

The cashier looked from her hair to her dirty fingernails as she asked for forty dollars on pump five. Charlotte's attention honed in on the posters behind him as he rang her up. *Please Help Find These People* was scrawled on a crumpled piece of paper taped above missing persons posters behind the register. She met her own eyes, centered on top of the many layers of posters. They had used that same beaming photo that she had found on Neil's phone.

She handed him the money and scurried out of the store. She pumped gas, tapping her foot rapidly as she waited.

What if I just call the police now? They'll be able to help me.

She looked around the gas station, waiting for the pump to click.

What if I'm not Charlotte? I just murdered a man.

She hoped no one could read her thoughts as she stared at her shoes, only they weren't really her shoes. They were probably a hiker's shoes as they were rugged and dirty. Probably a woman out hiking a beautiful Utah trail until she came across a house with broken windows and a man with a broken smile.

Probably a woman who Peter cooked to perfection.

Her stomach growled as she slipped back into the car, and as she drove out of the parking lot, a diner with flashing lights caught her eye. She pulled in, peering into the windows as she unbuckled. Sparsely seated people ate, each appearing more tired than the last. She fingered the wallet, counting out $351.

Should be enough.

She tucked the purse and shopping bag under the passenger seat and got out, struggling to lock the door with the old key. Feeling eyes on her, she looked into the diner, catching an older man staring at her.

Not another one.

She forced the key over, hearing the lock *clunk*, and jammed it into her pocket. Pasting a mean scowl on her face, she walked up the steps to the diner. Smells of cigarettes and burnt coffee engulfed her; all the while, every pair of eyes landed on her just through the doorway.

She didn't attempt a nervous smile or push her eyes to the ground. She walked with her head held high, catching eye contact with some of the other patrons. She sat down at a booth, rubbing her tired eyes. When she opened them, no one faced her. She relaxed into the seat as the waitress brought over the menu.

"What'll you have to drink?" she asked, emanating the scent of grease, sweat, and cheap perfume.

"Water and the strongest coffee you got," Charlotte answered, looking over the menu.

"You got it, hon. You look like you need it."

As the woman spun around, Charlotte said, "Hey."

The woman looked back at her.

"What are the waffles like?" She looked up to the waitress, feeling the weight of her eye bags dragging her down.

The waitress pulled her lip to the side. "They're fucking waffles." She spun back around, saying over her shoulder, "What're you new here?"

Charlotte watched her strut off until her eyes locked on the large TV on the wall above the bar. She read the captions, unable to hear the news anchor.

—*at Neil Ridges' home in Green River, Utah where Bethany Ridges, originally Bethany Free, has been found. Sadly, her body was retrieved from a fresh plot in the couple's front yard.*

Charlotte's focus fell on the plot behind the reporter, then back to the captions.

Found only feet above her body was Ramona Griffin. On-site forensics teams have determined Ramona's body was buried only days ago, while Bethany Ridges' body was buried weeks ago.

Bethany gasped.

I'm not Bethany.

Bethany remembered the drive here after the meal with Peter, sitting in the back of her own head like a passenger in her own body.

Tears ran down Charlotte's cheeks as Bethany ran to the bathroom. She locked the door behind herself, running her hands through her chopped hair. Looking in the mirror only caused her heartache.

Who am I?

Charlotte cried into her hands, the force of her tears crushing her chest. *Did I kill Bethany?*

Bethany kicked over the garbage can, her wet, red face contorted in agony. *I'm Bethany.*

I never felt like Neil's wife.

But I am.

Neil's purple face flashed in Bethany's mind. *I was.*

Charlotte shook her head. *I'm Charlotte.*

Bethany pulled at the hair she hated so much. *I hated Neil, but he was my husband and I was his wife. You don't even know who Charlotte is. You don't even know who you belong to.*

Charlotte crouched down next to the toilet, ready to heave. *Do you remember who you were before a few days ago?*

Bethany stood up and paced. *No.*

Charlotte held her head in both hands, squeezing as a hot knife plunged through her skull longways.

Bethany is dead.

I'm Bethany.

Bethany is dead!

I'm Bethany!

BETHANY IS DEAD!

I'M BETHANY!

A knock came from the bathroom door. "Ma'am, are you alright?" the waitress called.

Charlotte clamped a hand over her mouth, forcefully nodding. Between her fingers, she said, "Yeah." She doused her face in cold water, hastily drying it with rough paper towels. No one looked at her as she slid back into the booth.

A couple stood on screen, crying. Charlotte hesitated, her eyes finally dropping to the captions.

—ing our baby home! Charlotte is not your plaything, Neil! They'll find you!

Bethany snickered. *Not alive.*

Charlotte shook her head. The couple on the screen felt so unfamiliar. *I can't go home.*

"Figure out what you want?" the waitress asked, suddenly at her side.

Charlotte flinched. "Hey—uh—yeah. The Ranch House Mix."

"That's a lot of food for one girl."

Bethany glared up at the woman. "You heard what I said."

The waitress puckered her lips, her thin, drawn-on eyebrows raising, and took the menu. She waddled back to the kitchen, shaking her head.

Charlotte sipped her coffee, staring at the screen.

"More developments to come on the search for Neil Ridges and Charlotte Brenegan."

She watched as the segment changed to lighter subjects, the images simply passing by her eyes as her own matters took root deeper in her mind.

The waitress dropped off her plate.

Charlotte idly said, "Thank you," her eyes unmoving from the flashing images. She lifted her fork, finally eyeing the scrambled eggs. Poking them, she watched as they jiggled. Her skin prickled with the feeling of watchful eyes. She looked up, making eye contact with the waitress, who dove into the kitchen. Still having the feeling, Charlotte scanned the room, catching the eyes of the older man that had been staring at her outside.

She looked down at her eggs, taking a scoop and poking it with her tongue. Hastily, she shoved them into her mouth, and with a grimace, she chewed. They quickly found their way back onto her plate. She knew she should've gotten them fried. She prodded at the hashbrowns, taking a forkful with caution. They exited her mouth just as quickly as they had entered.

She sighed, picking up the toast.

Peter's voice echoed through her mind. *Good doggy!*

She took a bite of the toast, content.

Having only eaten the two pieces of toast, and not wanting to hear the waitress's mouth, Charlotte left forty dollars under the plate and scooted out of the booth. She tucked her wallet into the band of her skirt, noticing the older man was gone.

At the front entrance to the diner was a stand with maps of Nevada. She swooped one up, scurrying out to the parking lot.

Out in the beating sun, a voice called to her. It growled, imitating a cat, and keeping his gravelly voice low, the caller said, "What's up, Pussycat?"

Bethany turned around, a hand on her hip. She gave a smile and said, "Hmm?"

The man from the diner returned the smile, exposing tobacco-stained teeth. "I know a lot lizard when I see one."

Bethany didn't understand, her smile faltering.

"Get in my semi if you want some spending money." He winked and walked off to a cherry-red semi with a sleeper cab.

Bethany's smile returned, and so did PussyKat. She strutted over to his semi, opening the door and slipping in. The smell of B.O. smacked her in the face, but she remained calm.

"The name's Rick, but you can call me *Daddy*." Rick lay sprawled out on the bed at the back of the cab. The small curtains were drawn shut on his windshield and side windows, keeping what Bethany was sure was garbage on the floor in the dark.

She crawled over the passenger seat and onto the bed, immediately sticking her hand in something wet. To keep from showing her disgust, she asked, "How did you know they call me PussyKat?"

"That's just what I call all the lot lizards. Now shut up and take your clothes off."

Bethany propped herself on her knees in front of him, sliding her hand up his meaty thigh. "How about you go first?" She stopped her hand by his hip. She leaned in close and whispered, "Take your T-shirt off."

He grinned, eagerly pawing at his shirt. Pulling it over his head, his exposed rolls of pale-white, tender flesh. As he slid his arms out and lifted the shirt over his face, Bethany snatched a knife from the sheath slung around his belt and slashed his throat. He fell over, his weight shaking the whole truck as blood poured freely from his neck. His hands fought to hold pressure on the wound as his mouth sucked in the T-shirt over his face.

Bethany reveled in his moans and gurgles, excitement tingling her whole body.

As he stilled, she peeked over the T-shirt, looking into his dead eyes.

Charlotte smiled, the bloody knife in her hand screaming for her to put it to use. Grabbing the lunchbox Bethany spotted on the way in, Charlotte opened it and dumped out the contents.

She clutched the meat of his belly, fileting open the skin. Yellow sacks of fat dangled from the open flesh. Charlotte cut a few free, dropping them into the lunchbox.

Arching her back as she raised the blade above her head, she thrusted it into his chest, sawing downward. She dug her fingers in, pulling apart his chest cavity until the bones snapped and opened his body up like a book. She'd never felt so powerful. Charlotte sawed at the meat near the broken ribs, cutting off an entire rack. She cut these down into smaller sections, stuffing them all into the lunchbox until it almost couldn't zip closed.

Using his shirt, she cleaned off the blood on her hands and the lid of the box.

She hummed as she hopped out of his truck, skipping to her car. The key slid into the door lock easily this time. Charlotte hopped in, tossing her lunchbox into the backseat. She left the parking lot quickly, finding the nearest onramp in the direction she thought gave way to California.

Cars drove alongside her on the freeway, each giving her strange glances, at least, in her head they were. She slipped the map out from the band of her pants. Her fingers slid around on the slick paper, unable to unfold it as she steered with her knee. Tossing it aside, she decided she could read the signs as they came.

As the excitement of the score wore off, she realized how tired she was. Her stomach ached, longing for a bit of *Daddy*, and the back of her head throbbed. She pushed herself another painful hour up the highway before pulling off in a small town.

She drove down the main street, passing shops and bustling people in hopes of finding a less-populated area. A few turns later, she found herself surrounded by twitching folks who spoke to themselves and people camped out in tents on the sidewalk. It was the perfect place for her to blend in. She pulled into the parking lot of a park, having spotted the dilapidated grill from down the street.

With clumsy hands, she searched the purse she had hid under the seat, quickly finding a lighter. Lunchbox, lighter, and keys in hand, Charlotte made a run for the small barbeque. She took a few handfuls of bark from the playground and tossed them in, using a dry leaf to start the fire. The woodchips burned unhappily, barely staying lit until she rustled them around.

When the flames touched the grill, she threw four ribs on. Her mouth watered as she watched the flames tenderly lick the coagulated meat.

A sound came from the bushes, and a homeless man presented himself.

Charlotte looked down at the ribs, keeping her eyes from him. She tipped them over with the tip of the knife she kept as a keepsake, listening to them sizzle.

"'Scuse me, ma'am?"

She sighed, turning around with the knife in hand.

He eyed the blade clutched in her tight fist, stepping back once before saying, "D'you think you could share?"

She glanced over her shoulder at the meat and smiled. "Well, I don't think I'll eat all of these myself."

The man's cracked lips spread into a grin as he stepped closer to the grill. They watched the meat cook in silence, the smell torturing the duo.

Charlotte looked around at the drab houses around the park, catching the occasional pair of eyes from a passing bicyclist or driver. The sun cast pink rays through the clouds as the day ended. Crickets chirped through the chill air.

As she flipped over the ribs one last time, the man spoke. "Why does a life alone move slower than a life lived with others?"

She looked up to him, responding softly as to not disturb the world around them. "I'm not sure."

"The weight one carries alone is enough to end a man entirely."

Charlotte nodded. "I see your point, but what if others put more weight onto you?" Neil's snarl flashed behind her eyes.

He smiled. "Well, then, you may be surrounded by others but still utterly alone, and that's the worst kind of pain a person can experience."

She sighed, thinking, *I don't think it's quite the worst.*

"Although there are those that inflict pain on others, they themselves are in the most pain."

She nodded, wishing the ribs would cook so he could go away and stop rambling in her ear.

"People are selfish. They have needs that rely on others, and when those aren't met—"

"Oh, look, I think they're done!" she chirped, grabbing one and taking a bite. Grease dripped down her chin as her teeth sank into the flesh. *Daddy.* She smirked, handing the man a rib of his own.

He greedily took it, instantly putting it to his lips. Chewing, he inspected the rib, rotating it this way and that. "What kind of meat is this?" he asked.

Her smirk blossomed into a smile. She licked away the char stuck between her teeth, chuckling.

"Is," he paused, his eyebrows lifting, "is this pork?"

She remained silent, staring at him.

"It's not—" He paused, disgust contorting his face. "Is this human?"

"Would it make any difference to a starving man?" Charlotte shrugged, grease dripping onto her chest.

He gasped, dropping the rib onto the pavement.

"Aw, come on, man, that was hard to come by!" she yelled as he scuttled back to his place in the bushes. With one clamped between her teeth, she threw the rest of the cooked ribs in with the raw meat, zipping up the lunchbox as she ran back to her car.

Unlocking her door with one hand, she slipped in. She ripped a chunk of meat from the bone and started the car. Flicking on the headlights, she noticed only the right one worked. The car roared as she backed out of the parking space, slammed it into drive, and sped off.

Down a few streets, she spotted an abandoned theater. The cream masks of Thalia and Melpomene at the top of the theater shone in the moonlight. Its front doors were boarded up, along with the windows that covered its many floors. Charlotte glided into the parking lot, choosing a spot dead center. Finished with her first rib, she rolled down her window and tossed it out. The clatter echoed through the night as the bone bounced into the next parking space. She rolled up the window and dove into her lunchbox, snatching both the ribs. Holding one in either hand, she tore into them, gnashing her teeth as she chewed.

The cleaned bones made her sad, but her stomach was full. She tossed them out the window, wiped her hands on her pants, and hit the locks. Clambering over the center console, she landed in the back seat. Dust puffed up around her, and she choked, waving her arm around. Slipping off her sweatshirt, she wiped down the back seat and windows. She balled it up and set it on the seat, spotting something brightly colored on the floorboard. Her fingers grazed its soft surface before she picked it up. Holding it up to the moonlight, she saw it was a plush beach ball. She thought about all the kids in Peter's freezer and how they got there.

Something moved in the corner of her eye. She ducked below the front seat, peering around the headrest.

A group of homeless people, all bundled in blankets and tarps, passed on the sidewalk.

Charlotte's mind wandered back to the man at the park.

Should've killed that old man, Bethany spat.

Nah. He's okay. He won't tell anyone.

You disgust me.

And you disgust me. Charlotte lay down, curling up in the backseat.

Eating humans is wrong.

Killing humans is just as wrong and only feeds my addiction.

You can't go home.

Charlotte sighed. *I don't remember them, anyway.*

She stared out the front window for a while, imagining the couple on the news. *They were crying for me. People I don't even know.*

She started in the middle of the night. The moon beamed in on her from the back window. She sat up, the remnants of her dream slipping from her mind. In that moment, she decided she needed to see her parents.

The masks of Thalia and Melpomene mocked her as she drove out of the parking lot, her one headlight illuminating her path back home.

The road passed under her quickly, the image of her parents ever present in her mind. She crossed the border between Nevada and California and stopped at the nearest rest stop.

While leafing through a pamphlet from a table near the vending machines, a young man about her age walked in. She felt his gaze despite knowing she looked like crap. She hadn't bathed in days, and her efforts to wash up in sinks went without notice as she was stuck in the same dirty clothes.

Some sort of instinct kicked in as she jutted her hip out and gave him a sideways glance. When she caught his eyes, she smiled, surprised to see him return it.

He walked by, saying nothing before slipping into the men's bathroom.

Bethany thought about following him in, maybe bashing his head into the toilet over and over until his brain oozed from his nose, when a family of four walked in.

Charlotte smiled at them, taking the map and skirting around to the parking lot. She hastened her steps on the sidewalk, keeping her head down. Pulling the key out of her sweatshirt pocket and scanning the lot for her car, she caught eyes with someone. They stared at her through a tinted window, their identity concealed.

It irked her that someone should stare so intently. Bethany flashed them the bird, throwing up both hands. She smiled and thrust them toward the starer, watching their eyes widen.

Charlotte laughed and ran to her car as they opened their door. She backed out of her parking space and sped out to the freeway without looking back.

At a gas station farther in California, Charlotte thought she saw a face she recognized. It was a strange feeling. She realized the man simply looked like Peter and was saddened that her memory only took her back that far. She was certain that hundreds, if not thousands, of people had affected her life in both good and bad ways, much like any other human being. If she could only remember.

As she drove through the busy highway, she reconsidered where she was headed. She didn't have an address, only a town.

Can I really find them?

Tears blurred her vision, but she drove on. Signs passed her, each with her hometown on it with a decreasing number. She started to sweat. *What if someone recognizes me?*

Glancing in the rearview mirror, she decided that might be harder than she thought.

The road stretched on and on until she finally arrived at the exit. Pulling off the freeway, she felt no sense of relief, no flood of memories all restored like she imagined she would. The place was just as foreign as any other. She passed a large mall, wondering if she had ever gone inside.

Well, I think I grew up here, so, I've had to have gone inside, right?

Her anxiety peaked as she drove by pedestrians. Each seemed to glare into her dirty car, staring at her disheveled hair and clothing.

She finally parked at a public park, finding it mostly deserted. Her stomach growled angrily, and as she reached back for her lunchbox, she noticed there were no barbeques.

Looking in at the raw meat, her taste buds tingled. Pulling out one of Rick's sacks of fat, Charlotte held it over her head like a grape and plopped it in onto her tongue. Room temperature, it melted in her mouth, juicy and chewy. She vigorously chewed, wondering if her teeth would ever cut through.

Her eyes scanned over the playground, and although she found the slide familiar, she figured it was due to its resemblance to the one at the last park. Its corkscrew shape was the same as every other one she had seen recently.

Having successfully chewed through part of the fat sack, she swallowed a chunk, feeling as it dragged down her esophagus. Halfway through, it got stuck.

Charlotte's eyes bulged. She got out of the car, dumping over her lunchbox and spilling the meat across the passenger seat and floorboard. Charlotte rushed for the water fountain, holding her throat and grunting.

The only other people in the park were a woman and her dog and an old man who was just leaving. The woman heard her, spinning around.

Charlotte dove for the water fountain, taking in a few sips of water. It sat on top of the fat, trying to slip down into her lungs. She bent over and coughed, sending water onto the pavement.

With the old man gone, the woman felt a responsibility to help. She hooked her dog's leash onto a bench and ran for Charlotte. "I'm going to try to help you!" she yelled, standing behind and wrapping her arms around her chest. She thrust her fists into Charlotte's abdomen, quickly doing it a second time.

Charlotte gasped for air, still clawing at her throat. Neil's strained face broke through the surface of her focus as the woman struck her a third time.

The fat dislodged, landing on the ground with a wet slap. Charlotte gasped, falling to her knees as the woman let go.

The woman crouched down beside her, rubbing a hand on her back and eyeballing the splatter. "You alright, hun?"

Bethany panted, her hand slipping to the handle of her knife. She quickly turned, grasping the woman by the side of the head. In one sweep, the blade pierced her eye. The woman gasped, spasming as she fell over.

Her dog, its leash having slipped off the bench, wandered in the grass, meandering to the other side of the park as Charlotte carved the woman's remaining eyeball from her face. A moment passed as she stared into the severed eye before she popped it into her mouth, crunching through the woman's baby-blue iris as a spray of salty juices danced on her tongue. It was bitter, but she enjoyed the flavor as someone might enjoy a cup of black coffee. When she got to the lens of the woman's eye, which felt much like a tendon in a steak, she separated this from the soft meat and slid it through her lips. She grasped this with her grimy fingernails and flicked it away.

Grabbing the woman's arm, Charlotte sliced a chunk of meat away from the bone. She took it, grasping it by the wrinkled skin, and ran back to her car. Licking the knife clean, she clutched it between her teeth and got in, leaving in a flash.

Her foot lay heavy over the gas pedal. She set the meat on the center console, blood trickling over and onto the carpet.

I hope I didn't know her.

Charlotte glanced in her mirror, catching a glimpse of herself. Eyes wild, hair in tumultuous waves, and blood trickling down her chin, Bethany whispered, *You're a monster.*

Charlotte ran the stop sign, her red teeth glimmering through her smiling lips.

And for the first time, I feel free.

Twelve

Hawaiian spice or sweet and spicy?

At a grocery store she found while aimlessly driving around, Charlotte picked through the barbeque sauces, curious what the difference between the two flavors would be. Having a good stash of cash left in her pocket, she tossed both into the basket.

Semi clean from another gas-station bathroom sink, Charlotte felt she blended in well enough. There was enough riffraff in the store that looked worse than her despite the dark, wet stains on her sweatshirt and the gouges in the back of her head.

She glanced over the meat section, dismissing the pork roasts and steaks with an upturned nose. Better cuts of meat awaited her on her floorboard of her car.

On the utensil aisle, she picked up a large knife and a pair of tongs. She liked how large the knife was, especially in comparison to her pocket knife. Smiling, she clipped the tongs twice before setting them in the basket. After that, in went a couple of gallons of water, paper towels, paper plates, and a small, portable grill.

She waited in line, shifting her weight from one foot to the other. Setting her things on the conveyor belt, the cashier laughed.

"Having a barbeque?" she asked.

Charlotte glared at her despite trying to soften her expression. She felt like asking, *Who wants to know, Cynthia?* The name popped into her mind before she read the woman's name tag. When Charlotte checked it, her heart dropped.

Cynthia stared at her, expecting a response. As Charlotte stared back, Cynthia got uncomfortable and started to scan the items instead.

Charlotte laughed, too late and too abruptly, making Cynthia jump. "Yes." She laughed again. "Yes, I am."

The woman gave her a strange look, nodding as she bagged.

Charlotte watched the total, pulling out almost exact change in hopes to pay as quickly as possible.

As Cynthia handed her the bags, she stared into Charlotte's eyes, her own narrowing. With a light smile, she said, "You look familiar."

Charlotte, about twenty pounds lighter than when she went on that date, the one she didn't remember, nodded and said, "I get that often." She turned to leave, tense. The woman said no more as Charlotte exited the store, but deep down she knew Cynthia knew something.

Maybe Cynthia isn't very smart, Charlotte wondered.

Or maybe she doesn't like you, Bethany snapped.

Charlotte rolled her eyes, but sitting in the driver's seat, she wondered, *How did I meet Neil?* For a reason Charlotte couldn't even begin to explain, Cynthia felt tied to her past in a close way, as if maybe they'd been friends or maybe Charlotte just frequented the store.

A car pulled in the parking space in front of her, the driver and passenger facing her. This interrupted her thoughts. The couple from the news got out as she stared at them.

She gasped, sliding down in her seat to hide behind the steering wheel. *I'm not ready for this.*

Starting her car, she pulled out of the space, realizing this was her chance to find out their address—her address. She pulled around, parking in a spot a few rows behind their car in hopes of staying out of their sight. Her hunger subsided as she waited for them.

The sun was setting on her hometown as she opened the barbecue sauces, squeezed a small amount out, and licked. Sweet and Spicy was *much* spicier than Hawaiian Spice, Charlotte came to find out.

She almost missed her parents leaving while screwing the cap back on her gallon of water. At the last minute, she saw their taillights passing by her as they left the parking lot. She started her car and followed at a distance.

The drive was much shorter than she expected. Down the block, in front of a school, and one left later, her parents pulled into a driveway. She continued down the street, unknowingly parking in front of a fire hydrant.

Her hands trembled, and she felt as if she was breathing through a straw underwater. She asked herself what she was going to do, but the answer was clear. She had to see them up close before she could meet them.

Getting out of her car, she closed the door lightly, not bothering with the lock. She didn't plan on staying long. Casually, she strolled down the sidewalk, resisting the urge to tiptoe. She felt no real connection to the suburban street, none more than any other street she had been on in the past few days.

Listening, she heard her parents say no words as they entered the house, bags in hand. She didn't know what to expect. Besides the tears they had shed, she didn't know anything about them.

Lights flicked on in the house as Charlotte walked up the yard, her shoes squishing in the muddy grass. She stepped onto the porch, again expecting a feeling of familiarity and finding none. She watched through the front window, hiding just off to the side of it.

They set the bags on the counter, emptying them out and putting the things away just as any other couple would. The pictures on the wall relayed feelings of joy, but the faces on her parents displayed exhaustion and absolute sorrow.

Who was I to them? Besides their daughter, of course, was I good or bad?

A boy came out from a room she couldn't see into. He appeared to be maybe fourteen years old.

I have a brother!

The three silhouettes in her mind filled with the three people in the kitchen. Her eyes wetted themselves as she scanned the front room. The picture she had seen many times online and in missing persons posters beamed from the wall closest to the fireplace. She didn't know whether to love or hate the face behind the glass.

Her parents hugged her brother, their embrace bringing a warm feeling for Charlotte.

"What are you doing?"

Charlotte spun around, facing a man with a baseball bat. He didn't recognize her despite having lived next to her for her entire life. Her eyes widened as he pulled the bat back.

Bethany snatched the knife from her waistline, charging the man.

He screamed, tripping over a turtle statue in the yard. She toppled on top of him, raising the knife high. She swung down as he blocked her arm with the baseball bat. Her other hand gripped the bat, forcing it down. Slowly, it found its way to the man's neck. Bethany straddled the man's abdomen. Swinging the knife to the side, she pierced his ribs. He screamed and shoved the bat against her, lifting her up as she pressed down harder. She ripped the blade free, slashing for his exposed neck. The bat smacked her arm away.

"*Damn it!*"

Bethany forced the bat down with both hands, lifting her body and planting her knees on it. She thrust downward, the bat landing on the man's neck. His legs flailed as he tried to push upward. Finally balanced, Bethany stabbed the blade into his temple, burying it deep inside his brain. She watched him spasm like the old lady, his dark eyes crossing before he lay still.

Charlotte pulled the bloody knife from his skull with force, scooting just off his chest and onto his lap. All memories of her family, of the fact that she was at their front door, were gone, overlapped by the tumultuous wave of *need*. Both she and Bethany felt the grip of sickening excitement. Having done this before, she felt soaring confidence like none other. The blade dove into his chest, and Charlotte carved toward herself, sawing up and down. Panting, she ripped his chest cavity open with her hands, watching his heart throb in the moonlight. She slipped her fingers past his lungs and gripped the slippery flesh. It convulsed as she pulled it closer. Her mouth opened, embracing the warmth of his still-beating heart. She sank her teeth into the tough muscle, the writing meat spraying blood onto her tongue.

A beam of light fell onto her as her front door opened.

"*Charlotte?!*" her father asked, keeping her mother and brother back in the house with his arm.

Charlotte chewed the grainy flesh, blood pouring down her front. Looking up at them, she smiled and nodded. "It's me, Dad. I'm home."

Afterword

I wrote this book in 2021. It took me four years to finally rewrite bits of it and publish it. I was so nervous people would perceive my portrayal of multiple personalities as making fun of people with DID or similar disorders. The film *Split* faced lots of backlash for portraying someone with multiple personalities as a monster, but rereading my original manuscript four years after writing it, I realized Charlotte wasn't a monster. She's just a girl trying to survive.

Having Graves' disease has been the hardest thing in my life, even harder than the losses and abuse I've endured. Cycling on and off of anti-thyroid drugs is the most difficult. Having done so for the past eight years, I know I experience life with two different personality types. When I'm on my meds, I'm very withdrawn, down, without spark, and okay with being passive. When I'm off my meds, I'm extremely outspoken, emotional, full of that creative spark and passion, and driven. If you follow me on social media, you might even be able to tell when I'm on or off my meds based on what content I'm putting out. *I* can see it, but I'm not sure if the average viewer can.

Charlotte is an expression of the fear I have of losing myself to the meds. The anticipation I feel knowing I've relapsed (which can happen randomly no matter how well I take care of myself) and knowing I'll be put back on the meds is enough to shake me to my core.

Bethany is an expression of the anger I feel. The anger I feel towards my body for failing me; towards the doctors for not knowing more; the people I love for the smallest things. Irritability is not something I'm proud of.

HOME is also my way of expressing being a young woman with a hormonal disorder in the dating scene. When people feel entitled to your entire being, like they can mold you to their perfect image, a monster is bound to be born.

Thank you for spending some time in my head.

-Alyanna Poe
November 26th, 2025

Born in 2001 in California, I started my first novel at 14 and self-published it at 18. My writing journey was unexpected. What started as a form of expression turned into a way of life. I began sharing my stories with people and got addicted to connecting with readers around the world.
Thank you for being one of them.
You can check out my other books here:
authoralyannapoe.com
And follow me on Instagram where I post cannibal fun facts:
@authoralyannapoe
Thank you for believing in my work. I hope you enjoyed HOME, and even if you didn't, please leave an honest review on places like Amazon, GoodReads, and your social media.
Every review helps, even the ones talking shit! XD

Photo circa 2025 by Alyanna Poe

www.ingramcontent.com/pod-product-compliance
Lightning Source LLC
Chambersburg PA
CBHW021426200626
46814CB00015B/1553